Praise for *Better Living Throu*

Shortlisted for the 2011 Scotiabank Giller Prize

"[*Better Living Through Plastic Explosives*] shows the short story form at its savage best, each story capturing, with brilliant economy and grace, not only entire worlds but whole mindsets as they explode into eloquence. Gartner is one of the supreme noticers in contemporary fiction, and with this book she has produced a rare work of wisdom and laughter."
—2011 Scotiabank Giller Prize Jury

"Gartner has outdone herself with *Better Living Through Plastic Explosives*. She will garner a fistful of award nominations, more than a few fireworks, and maybe even some hang-up phone calls." —*Winnipeg Free Press*

"These stories ... thrum with bizarro life, the glowing bastard fruit of irradiated breeding experiments involving the DNA of a meticulous, fact-mad journalist, a snarky critic of hippie/hipster/Yuppie mores, an inventive stylist, and an old-school fabulist." —*The Globe and Mail*

"[A] superb new story collection. [Gartner] is the anti-Munro ... The emotional weight of Gartner's stories comes from the contrast between the persistence of uncontrollable biological urges and an artificial universe." —*National Post*

"[Gartner] drills into your brain with amazing images and a snappy delivery that verges on inciting mental whiplash. What a ride! ... Gartner is fall-out-of-your-chair funny, but the hilarity has a splendid whack of asperity to it for a great combination.

The ten stories in this book are wonderfully various and humorously satirical ... Her send-up of idiotic earnestness is so refreshing, I can't wait for the next collection."

—*The Vancouver Sun*

"With her second collection of short stories, Zsuzsi Gartner has delved far underground, taken its seismic measure, and returned to give us the report ... Dark, sinister, scary? Yes, but Gartner's skill in the telling is thrilling. I'm a new fan of Gartner. I really liked *All the Anxious Girls on Earth* ... But in *Better Living Though Plastic Explosives*, Gartner goes darker, deeper, and funnier. Her new stories are more trenchant, more satirical, more surreal. At the same time, Gartner still manages to evoke great empathy for characters and their sad, sad lives. Reading this book, I despaired ... But I also felt exhilarated, the same exhilaration I felt when first reading Vonnegut and Barthelme and, more recently, George Saunders."

—*Winnipeg Review*

"Zsuzsi Gartner's writing is dazzling, effortless, and clear as a bell. She's able to crystallize a cultural moment in a way entirely her own that is both instantaneous and eternal. I couldn't let go of it and read it all in one go."

—Douglas Coupland, bestselling author of *Generation X*

"What crazy, wonderful writing this is—hilarious, exuberant, apocalyptic, heart-stopping. Gartner sees all, dissects all, loves all. An absolutely irresistible collection."

—Barbara Gowdy, bestselling author
of *The White Bone* and *The Romantic*

Praise for *All the Anxious Girls on Earth*

"Zsuzsi Gartner is a brilliant, ball-busting, mid-expanding writer, the kind who sneaks up on you with her darkness, her wit, her imagination, her humour, her political savvy."
—*The Globe and Mail*

"Gartner writes smart, delicious fiction ... Consider it double espresso for the soul." —*Vancouver Courier*

"Zsuzsi Gartner's collection is better than great. The language dances on the pages." —*Calgary Herald*

"In every paragraph of this book there's genius."
—*Monday Magazine* (Victoria)

"The collection marks the entrance of a bold, challenging, entertaining writer, a rare crossbreed on any literary landscape." —*Now* magazine

"*All the Anxious Girls on Earth* is madly engaging and utterly accomplished. Like Lorrie Moore or Mary Flanagan, Gartner skilfully renders her anxious girls with both sadness and joy. Equal parts malevolent wit and great tenderness, these stories are original and reckless, and, like chocolate grasshoppers, are best swallowed whole."
—Lynn Crosbie, author of *Pearl* and *Liar*

"A combination of wicked humour, wild imagination, mordant satire, close observations, and tight, tight control."
—*Georgia Straight*

PENGUIN

BETTER LIVING THROUGH PLASTIC
EXPLOSIVES

ZSUZSI GARTNER is the author of the critically acclaimed and bestselling story collection *All the Anxious Girls on Earth* and the editor of *Darwin's Bastards: Astounding Tales from Tomorrow*. She is the winner of a 2007 National Magazine Award for Fiction and the recipient of numerous awards for her magazine journalism. Her second collection of short stories, *Better Living Through Plastic Explosives*, was shortlisted for the 2011 Scotiabank Giller Prize. She lives in Vancouver.

www.zsuzsigartner.com

STORIES

BETTER LIVING THROUGH PLASTIC EXPLOSIVES

ZSUZSI GARTNER

PENGUIN
an imprint of Penguin Canada

Published by the Penguin Group
Penguin Group (Canada), 90 Eglinton Avenue East, Suite 700, Toronto, Ontario, Canada M4P 2Y3
  (a division of Pearson Canada Inc.)

Penguin Group (USA) Inc., 375 Hudson Street, New York, New York 10014, U.S.A.
Penguin Books Ltd, 80 Strand, London WC2R 0RL, England
Penguin Ireland, 25 St Stephen's Green, Dublin 2, Ireland (a division of Penguin Books Ltd)
Penguin Group (Australia), 250 Camberwell Road, Camberwell, Victoria 3124, Australia
  (a division of Pearson Australia Group Pty Ltd)
Penguin Books India Pvt Ltd, 11 Community Centre, Panchsheel Park, New Delhi – 110 017, India
Penguin Group (NZ), 67 Apollo Drive, Rosedale, Auckland 0632, New Zealand
  (a division of Pearson New Zealand Ltd)
Penguin Books (South Africa) (Pty) Ltd, 24 Sturdee Avenue, Rosebank, Johannesburg 2196,
  South Africa

Penguin Books Ltd, Registered Offices: 80 Strand, London WC2R 0RL, England

First published in Hamish Hamilton hardcover by Penguin Canada,
a division of Pearson Canada Inc., 2011
Published in this edition, 2012

  2 3 4 5 6 7 8 9 10 (WEB)

Copyright © Zsuzsi Gartner, 2011

Author representation: Westwood Creative Artists
94 Harbord Street, Toronto, Ontario M5S 1G6

Please see page x for an extension of this copyright page.

LIBRARY AND ARCHIVES CANADA CATALOGUING IN PUBLICATION

Gartner, Zsuzsi
  Better living through plastic explosives : stories / Zsuzsi Gartner.

ISBN 978-0-14-317767-8

  I. Title.

PS8563.A6747B48 2012   C813'.54   C2012-900055-8

Visit the Penguin Canada website at **www.penguin.ca**

Special and corporate bulk purchase rates available; please see
www.penguin.ca/corporatesales or call 1-800-810-3104, ext. 2477.

ALWAYS LEARNING   PEARSON *for John and Dexter*

PLANET B

CONTENTS

SUMMER OF THE FLESH EATER

Field Notes on the Tendency of Varieties to Depart Indefinitely from the Original Type

—AFTER ALFRED RUSSEL WALLACE

Understand that pity is not what we're looking for. We are men, we remind each other as often as we can, and we must bear that burden. Forgetting was what got us into trouble in the first place. It's a weak word, *trouble*. But that's what came to mind when someone finally bought the Wong-Campeau place at the south end of the cul-de-sac. Stefan Brandeis took one look at the silver Camaro Z28 in the driveway and said, "Vroom, vroom. Here comes trouble." He was kidding, of course. Who could have believed that a barbarian was at the gates?

Their agent had priced the property before the market started to clench, but with their Ritalin-infused twins at Jean-Baptiste de Lamarck, an International Baccalaureate school we knew doubled as a rehab centre, the Wong-Campeaus couldn't afford to come down. That kind of corked-up familial stress inevitably manifests as fault lines. In other words, 2781 Chatham Close was, as Trevor Masahara succinctly put it, looking like crap. Marcus van der Houte had offered to fluff their place at a generous discount, but the W-Cs declined. (*Fluff* is not a term Marcus himself would use. His business card reads *Art Direction for Real Estate*.)

"I should've done it gratis," Marcus later said, more than once, more times than might have been necessary, while draining the last of another shaker of his signature fig-infused vodka martinis. "A couple of orange PVC Rashid pieces out front"—one of us, possibly Karlheinz Jacobsen, observed that the designer's cordless Dirt Devil was an "isomorphic miracle"—"and the door in Shade-Grown Espresso with a Spa-Blue casing to make the brown really pop …" All we could do was reassure him that he could hardly be held responsible for all that had happened. Or *caveat emptor*, as Patel Seth, our Latin scholar, put it.

"Damn his carnivorous soul to hell!" Kim Fischer had yelled from atop his carport towards the end, brandishing his fists like an Old Testament patriarch or modern-day mullah. It's perhaps not fair to speak of Kim, who with his unisex name and dubious tenor no doubt had more to contend with than the rest of us. His resilience was something to marvel at, though. We like to think he's running a raw-food retreat somewhere in the West Kootenays, or way out east, the Gatineaus maybe, remarried to a woman who appreciates his way with a paring knife, who understands that taking a pumice stone to the rough skin of your heels does not necessarily make you any less of a man.

But this isn't about Kim. You could say this is about evolution. You could say we've developed a deep personal appreciation for Darwin, the man and the theorist—his dyspeptic stomach, his human frailties, his ability to cling to contradictory desires. We've weighed anchor aboard the *Beagle*, if only in our dreams, charted our own Galapagos of the soul and found it wanting.

He moved in on the Canada Day long weekend. As the children circled the cul-de-sac on their Razors and Big Wheels, like planes stacked in a holding pattern, he arrived with a U-Haul hitched to the Camaro and started unloading. No moving company, just him. He wore what's commonly referred to as a muscle shirt but what some would call a wife beater. Stefan Brandeis noted that he hadn't seen a grown man in cut-offs that tight since Expo '86. (We later had a spirited debate about whether his was in fact a conventional mullet or ersatz hockey hair.) The first thing wheeled out of the U-Haul was a hulking, jerry-built barbecue. He seemed friendly enough. He flashed what Trevor Masahara called "a big, shit-eating grin" at those of us who'd gone over to welcome him with a pitcher of iced Matcha tea spiked with Kentucky Gentleman.

"Shake hands with the Q," he said, patting the hood of the barbecue as if it were a loyal hound, the half moons of his prominent cuticles edged in grease. Karlheinz Jacobsen's wife later commented that he smelled a bit ripe, and the other women made a show of fanning the air in front of their faces. Kim Fischer's wife even enthusiastically snuffled Kim's exfoliated pits like a truffle pig. At the time it seemed they were being a trifle judgmental, but one thing we'd always appreciated about our wives was that they spoke their minds.

It bears mentioning that he did something else that first day as we gathered around his "Q" trying to make small talk. Without missing a beat, he reached down to rearrange himself inside his cut-offs. This is something we've never talked about, not even Stefan B. Some things are better left unannotated.

Afterwards, he sat down on his new front steps and drank beer straight from the can, wiping his lips with the back of his hand, exaggeratedly rotating his shoulders as if attempting to recalibrate himself. It had all been amusing at first, some kind of sideshow. Like having a Molson ad shot on your very own street. This was before the dog arrived, and the Dodge one-ton.

That day is easy to recall with a great deal of clarity for another reason. We'd always been spared the smell from the rendering plant across the Burrard Inlet. But on July 1, there occurred a shift in the wind that continued unabated throughout the summer. The congealed odour of pyrolyzed animal parts would enter the cul-de-sac and then just hang there, as if snagged on a hydro line. It came and went, some days thankfully better than others. *Can you smell it?* we'd ask hopefully at the gelato shop two blocks away on Mountain Highway. *Didn't you smell it on Albermarle Drive as well?* we quizzed our letter carrier, who took to pelting through her rounds on the cul-de-sac as if Cerberus were at her heels. It was difficult to believe we were the only ones in our North Vancouver enclave saddled with the almost gelatinous stink. There were days when even the leaves of the silver birches that edged the ravine behind our properties appeared to curl back from it. The cedars and the Sitka spruce, more stoic trees, stood their ground.

We have accepted our confluence of bad luck not as a "sign" of something, but rather for what it apparently was: bizarre coincidence. People have driven themselves insane for millennia trying to figure out "what it all means." Most often things just *are*.

"I know it's only a smell," Trevor Masahara said one particularly rank Tuesday evening, interrupting our book club's parsing of Clarissa's guilty rejection of the hydrangea in *The*

Hours, "but sometimes it seems like, you know, an actual *thing.*"

His name? It's easy to forget he actually had a name, a driver's licence, most probably a SIN. For a while we called him The Truck Guy and later The Meat Guy. Karlheinz Jacobsen, who has a scientific bent, was the one who nicknamed him Lucy. You know, the so-called missing link? We thought this was terribly funny. "Lucy," Stefan Brandeis would yell mock *sotto voce,* "you got some 'splainin' to do!" while the rest of us laughed. We literally yowled. It seems even then we had more in common with other animals than we could have imagined.

A couple of days after he'd moved in, as if it had been teleported there overnight, the Dodge Ram, circa early '80s, sat on blocks in the middle of his front lawn. Off-white (*tapioca,* Marcus van der Houte insisted), one broken headlight, and on the slightly dented back bumper a peeling orange neon sticker that read I'M GOING NUCKIN' FUTS! And one of those chrome Jesus fish. (We never did witness any signs of even covert religiosity, a disappointment to Karlheinz Jacobsen, who alone among us held to a notion of the divine.) The kids went giddy—instant ADHD—as if they'd never seen a truck before.

Marcus was the one who elected to go over to talk to him about it. Bear in mind that we didn't then, nor subsequently, ever use the term "property values." We are not the kind of men who fixate on our lawns. In fact, those of us with southern exposures have switched to drought-resistant native grasses. And if there is grass that needs cutting, a communal Lee Valley push mower is used.

He was underneath the truck banging around, bare knees poking out, feet in decaying Adidas. Marcus tapped out the end-credit sequence to *Moulin Rouge* on the hood to get his attention. (Marcus's ten-year-old son told him later, "You should've just yelled 'Yo!'") The slathering muzzle of what looked like an Alsatian/Cayman cross shot out of the front passenger window, and Marcus fell on his seersucker-clad ass, cartoon-style, white bucks up over his head. (For the record, at least one of us failed to suppress a guffaw.) The guy slid out from under the truck with a grunt while the dog continued its concerto.

He offered Marcus a greasy paw (our neighbour, not the dog) and heaved him up. After they "shot the shit for a while," as Trevor put it, our reconnaissance man gave a wave and walked away wiping at his grass-stained butt.

"I lost my nerve," Marcus said later. We assured him we would have as well, while Patel Seth pried his fingers from his third black mojito and suggested it might be a good time to up his dose of citalopram.

Fear, we all know, is a useful adaptation. "Only the brave die young," Stefan Brandeis said rather soberly, and for once it seemed he might not have been joking.

The dog's name was Gido. He wasn't a bad dog really, despite being seriously misbred, his gene pool a murky concoction that no doubt involved at least one AWOL chromosome. Contrary to what his owner might have desired, he did seem all bark and no bite. His oversized head, with its long snout housing teeth in double rows like a shark's, balanced on a dachshund's body. He looked alarmingly like a life-sized bobble-head dashboard dog. How he ever managed to hold up that head for any length of time we'll never know.

We can now admit an isolationist stance would have been best for all concerned. But we did what any civilized tribe would

have done under the circumstances and invited our new neighbour to a dinner party. The soiree was held at the Brandeis-
Lahr place, as they have the most accommodating deck. It was
one of those sultry, edge-of-the-rainforest evenings, but the
lingering smell from the last shift at the rendering plant soon
drove us inside. We were discussing what Trevor Masahara's
wife maintained was an apocryphal story about the worth of
a certain crowd-pleasing Egyptian Bastet cat statue at New
York's Metropolitan Museum when our guest of honour
arrived with a two-four under one arm, dressed in sweatpants
of some ambiguous vintage and, to everyone's relief, a T-shirt
with sleeves. He clamped a beer between his molars before
anyone could offer him a bottle opener and said something
like, "How is everyone?" (Patel Seth recollects it as the more
colloquial "Howz it hangin'?")

The cat statue, Kim Fischer continued, after a series of
ill-executed high-fives and faux gut punches initiated by our
new neighbour, turned out to be much too valuable an anti-
quity to be put on open display, so what museum-goers were
gaping at was in fact a meticulously wrought replica. When
this got out, no one was interested in viewing it anymore.
Karlheinz Jacobsen recalled the story differently—that the
actual statue *was* put on display, but after being authenticated
by a third-party expert on the Ptolemaic period was found to
be a fake.

"It's all the same in the end, isn't it?" said Patel. "People
place great stock in authenticity." He turned to our guest,
who stood squinting his eyes and chewing his upper lip as if
deeply considering the issue, and asked his opinion. "What I've
been wondering," he said, thrusting his beer in the direction
of Trevor's chest, "is how much mileage you get with that rice
grinder out there."

Kim's wife, ever diplomatic, extended a skewer of honey-glazed late-season fiddleheads, cultivated in the dankly shaded side of their house. "Kim's a committed locavore," Trevor said, recovering himself admirably. "He's been trying to convert us all." The Truck Guy smirked and twirled a finger alongside his right ear: "Loco what?" We had no choice but to laugh along good-naturedly, even Kim. He was our guest, after all, the new guy on the block.

The evening proceeded towards what could in hindsight be clearly seen as a preordained train wreck. ("In the land of the blind, the one-eyed jack is king," a hungover Stefan remarked the next morning. To which Trevor replied, "Come again?") Our neighbour actually giggled at Marcus's lamb popsicles in fenugreek sauce, and when Karlheinz unveiled a test-tube tray of plastic ampoules filled with wild-morel cream that we were meant to squirt into our mouths (the women loved it, that clever Karl!), he pretended to inject his *amuse bouche* into the raised veins traversing the waxy underside of his left arm, flexing in a manner that accentuated his already over-delineated bicep. Again we laughed. (Although Marcus stage-whispered to Patel, "It's obvious that he's never actually shot up.")

Karlheinz was explaining his failed attempts at crossbreeding golden agoutis with voles in order to create sleeker guinea pigs when someone passed our new neighbour a plate of Trevor's dulse salad. He demurred, muttering something about erectile dysfunction.

What felt like light years later, during which "Hot Rod" (as Stefan dubbed him that night) frequently interrupted the conversation with detailed descriptions of the modifications he'd made to his car—Noki adjustable shocks, Bruce Herb 1.31-inch anti-sway bar, two-inch lowered Simpson Michigan leaf springs[?], EJR carpet, Dyno-Mite insulation, restored dash pad, Ultra-Lite Automorphic gauges, Painfree Wire 16 circuit, '68–'74 muscle-car kit, TPS polygraphite bushings [?] used throughout, *including body mounts*, WRT Z28 coil springs, Calvert Johnson "Cal-Rac" traction bars [a pause for lubrication here], Black '73 interior, *added years ago!*, Sony Frost Mark stereo head unit, 5 × 160 watt amp. *And believe you me* a twelve-disc multi-play CD changer, two 6 × 9 Altitude rear speakers, and PH Quartz components in front—he returned bleary-eyed from yet another trip to the bathroom and shot dual pistol fingers at each of our wives. "Next weekend I'll make you ladies some real food."

With that he disappeared into the night, and in the elongated silence that followed we could hear the waters of Lynn Creek churning through the gorge below the water-pipe bridge as the snowpack far above melted in the July heat. Already it had claimed a young man, the season of playing chicken with the creek only just begun. We could almost *hear* the melt.

Sure, we knew men like him existed. But we'd never had a chance to observe one in such close proximity. Karlheinz confessed to thinking of him as a *specimen*, and we nodded in agreement.

We have often wondered what Darwin would have made of the summer-long struggle for existence on our cul-de-sac. If he'd lived here, would he have taken the role of observer or participant? By all accounts he was a bona fide gentleman, didn't partake of arguments, even kept his own counsel when the *Beagle*'s mad Capt. FitzRoy expounded at length during dinner—as if daring the naturalist to differ—on the Book of Genesis. (Once, only once, did he weigh in, when the captain was explaining the trickle-down benefits of slavery, proving our hero did have a backbone.) Did he float above the chickpeas and rice in the captain's mess, a benign smile shielding his face, lost in barnacle dreams? Did he clutch his stomach and plead seasickness and flee to his cramped quarters?

Something we can be certain C.D. didn't consider: reaching across the table and throttling FitzRoy until the man's eyes bulged from their sockets.

We found his backyard well-kept, albeit oddly quaint. ("Holly Hobbie chic," Stefan called it.) Garden gnomes stood here and there ("Gnomically," Patel later said, as if reciting a Zen koan rather than a bad pun) amongst towering delphiniums and various mulleins. Lobelia and other generic annuals spilled from a small weathered wheelbarrow, and a blown-glass hummingbird feeder hung from the coral bark maple.

Surely the W-Cs couldn't have left these things? But it was even more inconceivable that they belonged to him. (It now seems laughable that we wasted so much time over the following week debating the question of whether he had bought all this in earnest or whether he had an understanding of its kitsch value. Karlheinz had posited the most plausible theory: "It could be they were his mother's and he maintains them through a sentimental streak." That we could understand, although Marcus couldn't help reminding us that sentiment is anathema to design.)

The "Q" stood in the centre of the yard like a Mayan shrine in the cloud forest of Cobán, feathered in smoke and snapping and spitting as fat hit the fire. Mosquito torches on bamboo poles flanked the barbecue. (Trevor's wife deemed this "thoughtful.") The patio table was laden with platters of raw meat, the variety defying categorization, but our host was all too willing to lead a tutorial. There were slabs of porterhouse steaks, rib-eyes, short ribs, spareribs, pork loin chops, lamb shoulder chops, and lamb leg steaks. He eschewed terms like "well-marbled" in favour of "nice and fatty" and smacked his palm down soundly on cuts he deemed particularly "bodacious." We hardly need point out that there wasn't a rub or a marinade in sight.

REO Speedwagon blasted from what looked like car speakers attached to the balustrade of his deck. He later came strolling through the sliding doors with a guitar, yodelling "Ring of Fire" as a prelude to dishing up his Voodoo Chili, a recipe he had evidently learned in a squat on the outskirts of Port-au-Prince. He promised us his chili would fire up visions of Erzulie Dantor, the Haitian goddess of sex. She would make love to us in our dreams. His way of putting it of course involved more colourful terminology, in a dialect Patel, our own Henry Higgins, recalls as "Thunder Bay, 1977."

We will admit to the record that he was an attentive host that evening, exuding a kind of ruffian charm in his own milieu. He even kept his talk of body mounts and adjustable shocks to a minimum. It also bears mentioning that this was the closest we ever came to being chummy. At one point he and Trevor engaged in a tête-à-tête about the ultimate burger. (Trevor swears by a knob of frozen blue cheese encased in the centre of 275 grams of hand-chopped Kobe sirloin.) "No shit," he kept saying, sounding genuinely impressed as Trevor pulled out his BlackBerry to do some quick temperature conversions (our host not having mastered the move from imperial to metric back in grade school). "No shit."

It turned out that among his many adventures he'd spent some time in the Australian outback. "Kangaroo," he told us, "is a beautiful protein." Patel's wife, who is an ear, nose, and throat specialist, said she found that poetic. (A less generous person might have said, "She wouldn't know poetry if it bit her on the ass," but Patel wasn't that kind of guy.)

Other things we learned that night: Chicken isn't meat. Medium-rare is for chumps. Boys who can burp the Lord's

Prayer at age eight retain the ability, like a vestigial limb flaring to life, well into their thirties.

The night was alive with smoke and fire. Insects were held at bay. Blood pooled on his plate. Stefan's wife leaned forward and dragged a finger through it and then exaggeratedly sucked. At the time, we erroneously believed she was mocking *him*.

For a while after that, things were good. Almost too good. Kim's wife turned to him in bed the night of the barbecue and said, "Fee-fi-fo-fum, I smell the blood of an Englishman." He told us her overbite had glinted in the bedside light like the teeth of something feral. We all knew what he meant. Even Marcus's wife, who has a no-nonsense air about her and is an avid golfer, started running her fingers through her cropped hair in a manner some of us found disconcertingly attractive. (During those brief, heady days, more than one child walked in on a mid-afternoon scene in a rec room or kitchen that elicited hysterical giggles or cries of "Gross!")

We found it impossible not to notice that by the third week of July the hair on our neighbour's chest and shoulders looked thicker, more pelt-like than the springy bed of curls that had so freely dripped sweat the afternoon he moved in. Throughout the first half of the summer it seemed he was out there every day tinkering with the truck and later with the Ford Ranchero pickup that joined it on its own blocks on his front lawn. From time to time he'd wave to us with a monkey wrench or soldering iron. "Now that he's discovered fire," Stefan quipped one morning while squeezing into Patel's Mini Cooper with those of us who didn't telecommute or weren't on paternity leave, "maybe he's trying to reinvent the wheel."

His property became a magnet for the kids. They played in the trucks, roughhoused with Gido, abandoned their tennis racquets and unicycles and junior geologist kits in favour of slingshots and handmade blow-dart guns. ("This is how they kill in the Amazon!" Trevor's five-year-old informed us, adding that all they now needed were poison arrow frogs to toast over a fire like marshmallows, the venom oozing to the surface like a toxic froth.) They showed waning interest in the computer-animation camps, father-son mini-triathlons, and Urbane Kids Cook! classes we'd pre-enrolled them in months back. We feared they'd soon be running wild in Lynn Canyon, engaging in some kind of *Lord of the Flies* one-upmanship with rival cul-de-sac kids. They came around in the late afternoons saying they'd already had a snack "at Gido's," their breath redolent with the after-effects of processed meats and root beer, their eyes narrower than the last time we had looked closely at them.

Were we neglectful fathers? Were we secretly relieved to find more time on our hands after work and on weekends than we'd ever thought possible post-fatherhood? There was something in the still-childless Kim's eyes that made the rest of us feel guilty, but he never levelled any accusations. Kim was always the quiet one, the exemplar of those still waters they say run deep. Our wives assured us that unstructured time was what childhood summers used to be all about, but we couldn't help suspecting that their uncharacteristic nostalgia hinted at a buried desire to revert further into an idealized past.

Chas, as we've taken to affectionately calling Darwin, was understandably discomfited by the natives of Tierra del Fuego. In lean times, he was told, they would devour their grandmothers while sparing their dogs. He was apparently misled by a young trickster, as later reports dismiss the notion that the Fuegians were cannibals.

But why even think of this now? There are still grandmothers in the world and there are still dogs and there are places on earth where the former are abused and the latter venerated. And vice versa.

By early August the trucks stood neglected in his front yard and the Camaro seldom left the driveway. He now took his Harley Low-Rider everywhere—the deadening percussion of the altered muffler competing with the stench from the rendering plant for most-obnoxious-emission status. His favourite T-shirt—or at least the most frequently sported—read *Loud Pipes Save Lives*. Gido perched on the back, small ears flattened in the wind, happy as a gargoyle, roaring down Mountain Highway.

Plants better suited to the bogs of the Carolinas ("Or the late Cenozoic period," Stefan noted) began to spread across his property. Waxy-leafed vines twisted around the trucks, even creeping out through the exhaust pipes, their ropy tendons like the neck muscles of dehydrated bodybuilders. Moss bearded fenders and chrome grilles. Cobra plants and monkey cups and other flesh-eaters proliferated. Even dragonflies became ensnared, their death rattle unnerving. ("Like ice in a blender," Marcus observed, swirling the dregs of a kiwi-and-peppercorn daiquiri.) Giant hogweed ("*Heracleum mantegazzianum*," Karlheinz informed us, "with sap so toxic the skin reddens and blisters after contact before erupting in severe inflammation prone to infection") soon shot up well beyond the roofline. We finally had a non-negotiable reason to forbid the kids to play in his yard.

Trevor, who had gone into the backyard on the pretext of retrieving an errant Frisbee-golf disc, reported that it was almost swampy, as if the groundwater were rising. A crudely framed smokehouse hung with small carcasses was set up where gnomes had previously stood guard by the delphiniums. And behind the smokehouse, what could only be described as a midden of bones.

What our summer had been reduced to: endless speculation. Spying on a neighbour. (Karlheinz, in fact, had begun to compile *field notes*—"evidence," he called it.) Petitioning various city and provincial bureaucracies to do something about the at-times-unspeakable (and, we were told, *cross-jurisdictional*) odour infiltrating our cul-de-sac from the other side of the inlet. Our fitness regimens—let's just say we were finding it more and more difficult to confront a full-length mirror most days. Our joie de vivre felt as if it were being sucked out of us one pore at a time by a super-strength vacuum cleaner.

And from his backyard the continual haze of smoke rising.

Whenever we complained, about the noise, the smoke, the smell, the sheer onslaught of it all, our wives absent-mindedly stroked our hair (or, in Marcus's case, his aggressively shaved dome) as if petting cats, their thoughts, we assumed, on the demands their careers were making on their time. Our holiday plans were falling through, one after the other, collapsing due to inertia on our part and the fact that an unseasonable crunch time appeared to have hit the medical, legal, architectural, geological, and IT professions almost simultaneously. We're still not in complete agreement about whether we were twenty-first-century men for not questioning our wives' work commitments or whether we were dupes. (Trevor, ever self-flagellating, prefers the dupe theory. He is also the one who misses Kim the most.)

Our wives no longer arched close while we watched HBO late in the evenings, angling for a deep-tissue massage or core realignment. It transpired that more than one of them had faked orgasms on multiple occasions. Patel told us his wife had called the tantric sex workshop we'd all taken in the early spring "a joke." Marcus's wife declared that cunnilingus was meant only for lesbians and cats.

Our neighbour had taken to pulling the "Q" out onto his driveway in the early evening, dispensing goodies as if he were a hot dog vendor at the corner of Hornby and Robson. We could forbid the children from playing over there, but we certainly couldn't forbid our wives, who drifted over to sample his wares. Karlheinz actually witnessed him laying a piece of deeply charred something or other directly onto Kim's wife's extended tongue, as if proffering a communion host. Our wives would come home, often after the sun had set, talking about things like "honouring the whole beast," marrow smudges at the corners of their mouths.

It cannot be said we didn't pull out all the stops. We still maintain that "Operation Aphrodisiac" was executed flawlessly. Patel made his Lapsang souchong–smoked duck breast with pomegranate sauce. Kim made dolmades using grape leaves from his own garden. Then there was Karlheinz's oyster foam–filled agnolotti, Trevor's quail stuffed with raisins and quinoa, and Stefan's saffron risotto with truffle oil and mascarpone. Marcus's silky black cod with Pernod mole sauce (70 percent pure, fair-trade cocoa) filled the role of dessert.

Kim even booked himself a spa treatment. (We're still curious as to whether he went through with the rumoured "crack wax.") At the time, we accepted this as further evidence that he was the bravest and most evolved of us all.

[Our notes are sketchy at this point. Accounts vary too widely to be coherent.]

It was shortly after what Patel christened our Failed Feast of the Satyricon that our wives started dressing differently.

("Their slut phase," Trevor would later call it, reminding us how mutable this thing we call the "personality" really is.) At first we thought it was the dry heat, something none of us were used to. The day Kim's wife headed out to a pre-trial discovery dressed like Britney Spears's little sister, her Nunzia briefcase incongruous alongside the terry cloth short shorts and baby-T, we could no longer deny that some kind of deleterious mutation was taking place. For once we were glad we had only sons and no daughters.

We thought at the time that this was all to do with meat. Could too much unmediated animal protein cause a chemical disturbance in the frontal granular cortex, we asked Karlheinz, who simply shrugged. He was as lost by then as the rest of us, science no longer the bulwark against disorder that he had believed it to be. (Karlheinz had, by then, started attending Mass again.)

"I just don't see why meat has to be the main event!" Kim Fischer detonated one day, seemingly apropos of nothing. We nodded fervently, as if at a Free Methodist revival meeting. Someone, most likely Stefan, added, "Amen, brother!"

No one was yet speaking in tongues.

Then Gido killed Karlheinz's agoutis. That was the official story. The supposition, anyway. The hutches were open, the agoutis were gone. But, *nihil fomeus cannone*, Patel said, the best he could come up with in Latin for "no smoking gun." Without sufficient evidence ("Or balls," Trevor later said) we could not confront our neighbour. Not then.

We inspected the blood-smeared grass, stomachs contracting. We could smell murder. All day long the boys yelped in the ravine edging the backside of the cul-de-sac, something distinctly tribal in their ululations. The women, strangely, weren't disturbed by the carnage. They didn't even come by to check out the blood on the grass, which by the evening was thick with flies.

They told our children, "When animals kill each other we don't call it murder." Our lovely, brilliant, Darwinian wives.

We determined that the trapped smell, that wilful pong, was a result of a geo-architectural force, like the buffeting wind tunnel downtown created by the arched, open corridor to the Vancouver Public Library's northeast entrance. Trevor was all for cutting down the Sitka spruce grove that towered over the cedars and silver birches along the ravine. Although a couple of us wavered, we finally came down adamantly against. Those trees were not even our property. "But it's our stink, right?" Trevor maintained.

What we feared: Trevor, with his refined sense of smell, would go off his nut in the night and take a chainsaw to the trees.

The black-bear signs had been up for weeks. The dry summer caused sporadic wildfires farther up the North Shore Mountains, and no doubt berries were sparse. Whereas other kids learned to dial 911 at an early age, ours had committed to memory 604-990-BEAR. Lucy, as we were calling him by then, scoffed at the signs and the directive: *Remove all bear attractants (food)*. "Gido could take them out," he boasted. As if taking a bear out was what was required, as if our cul-de-sac were a kind of gladiatorial arena where a wandering cub and a Down's-afflicted mongrel could grapple to the death while we laid our bets.

Helicopters juddered by overhead almost daily. A fugitive was suspected of hiding on Mount Seymour, although he was later found in a tool shed near Indian Arm. A woman tossed

her child from the Capilano suspension bridge, but it miracu-
lously survived. Two Japanese exchange students wandered off
three-quarters of the way up the Grouse Grind arm in arm and
disappeared into the trees.

We no longer communicated with our children except
through a kind of sign language. They spoke in coded grunts and
shrugs. Stefan's twins talked to each other in clicks and clacks
of the tongue, like the bushmen of the Kalahari. They drew on
the garage walls with the charred ends of sticks and charcoal
briquettes as if drawing on the insides of caves—of the things
they imagined, or the things that had yet to happen, it wasn't
clear then. A small figure emerging from bushes on what looked
like an enormous turtle. Men with sharp implements converging
on a cowering beast. Tangles of foliage and fire. Rain.

Sightings of our neighbour became rare, his comings and
goings much less of a show, perhaps achieved under the cover
of darkness, the revving of the Harley less and less frequent,
until the bike was permanently dry-docked. Gido had such a
disappointed air about him that Karlheinz suggested taking
him for a ride on Marcus's Vespa so he could at least feel the
wind in his ears.

Stefan swore he had seen Lucy's arms swinging along, his
knuckles skimming the ground, pelvis tipped backwards as he
made his way through the dense overgrowth to his backyard
after depositing his garbage container by the curb. (His front
door obscured by a tangle of vines.) He was certainly moving
more deliberately now whenever we did see him, and wasn't as
quick with the rejoinders as he had been. It was only after he
stopped the clowning completely that we realized how much we
had enjoyed viewing him as a harmless throwback. Patel, who
is intermittently nocturnal and lives adjacent to him, claimed he

had seen Lucy on his haunches, eating raw meat straight from the carcass of some small creature. This only made Karlheinz scoff. "Neanderthals cooked meat on hot stones." We were touchy with each other by then.

Each of us had our own theories. Cro-Magnon! *Homo habilis! Homo erectus! Australopithecus robustus!* Our hypotheses flew back and forth like insults. We clung to these with a certainty that was all the more convincing for being feigned. Six blind men describing an elephant, when in fact the whole of a thing is so often not so much greater or lesser but completely different from the sum of its parts.

But why even trouble with taxonomies? They are shifty, after all, and, as we've learned, in the end it's all just words.

It was towards the third week of August that our wives started avoiding us altogether, disappearing into themselves as the sky fell. We tried following them, walking barefoot, careful on the tinder-dry pine needles underfoot, breathing through our mouths slowly and evenly. We knew this wasn't the way it was supposed to be, fire ants pouring from the peonies, keeping watch while our wives grunted among the vines. But they were always home by morning.

Right before the Labour Day weekend, one of the Japanese exchange students came up out of the ravine straddling the back of a giant tortoise. She looked dazed but otherwise unaffected, the tortoise heavy lidded and benign. (Stefan remarked that it looked a little like Sinatra in his later years.) It was Trevor who called 911. Only after the emergency vehicles and media people that converged on the cul-de-sac had gone did we realize that no one had thought to take a photograph. The ones in the newspapers and on SnapTweet, and the footage on the news and on YouTube, didn't come close to capturing the other-worldliness of what we had witnessed. The aquarium issued a statement that a tortoise recently acquired for its upcoming Galapagos exhibit had indeed gone missing from its transport container. But we still wonder.

The boys had jostled for proximity to the tortoise, prodding it with sticks despite our entreaties. One of them (Marcus's son?) even poked at the girl. By that point a kind of despair permeated our cul-de-sac. Only our sons seemed oblivious to the smell and the frequent volcanic eruptions that pockmarked our driveways with small craters. We had prided ourselves on raising children with a high emotional IQ, but these little creatures had become alien to us, and we could only watch them from an increasing distance as if from the reverse end of a telescope.

Our wives squatted on their haunches in front of backyard fires they'd built in pits lined with basaltic rock, looking at us with those eyes, waiting for us to do something. Hunt? Gather? Or something else, something beyond our capabilities altogether?

We're aware that by today's standards the retiring Chas himself would have been considered a bit of a barbarian by some. He collected specimens by the thousands and thought nothing of casually slitting open the bellies of creatures to examine the contents of their stomachs. On the Galapagos he made a sport, under the guise of research, of swinging a lizard by the tail and hurling it out over the water as far as he could. He caught the terrified creature as it crept back onto the volcanic shore and catapulted it again and again. This type of lizard could evidently swim but was afraid of water. What the naturalist deemed this contradiction: apparent stupidity.

On Labour Day, Kim's wife left. Patel, not generally a man to talk in clichés, later kept repeating, *Thank God there were no children*, and not one of us even considered scoffing. She had gone not to Lucy's as we'd first suspected, but clear across the bridge to another life that was not to include Kim. This was all in her note. (It has to be said, now that Kim is no longer here, that we were taken aback by her schoolgirlish handwriting and her choice of stationery.) All of us were in agreement about whose fault this really was.

Late that night we were decidedly sombre as we gathered in Kim's kitchen, lit only by the amber glow of LED pot lights. To get through the dense foliage, we would have to take the equivalent of machetes to the vines and the thick-ribbed hogweed stalks. Kim doled out fully forged and polycarbon-tipped chef's knives with military precision. How different those Sabatiers and Wüsthofs were from the stone tools we found scattered around our ancestor's backyard. We buried those as well. (Stefan has confessed to pocketing a Mousterian scraper as a souvenir, although we agree *souvenir* seems the wrong word. Patel suggests *memento mori*.)

Lucy, you got some 'splainin' to do! How could he have explained? With that jaw grown so heavy it was now only good for mastication? With that tongue that most of us were certain had nimbly traced figure eights on our wives' breasts and thighs, now thickened and barely contained in the bowl of his mouth? Trevor swears he pleaded. His eyes, buried under that shelf of brow, begged for understanding. Did he plead? Sometimes even the merest suggestion of what may have happened is enough to make you question your own recollections.

As for Gido, what could we do? That dog had an exceptional sense of smell. And halfwit or not, that dog was loyal.

Even now we're not ashamed to admit that more than one of us wept. Karlheinz the longest and hardest.

The mail continues to arrive at 2781, the bills get paid, even the mortgage, thanks to Trevor's computer-hacking skills. Come tax time Stefan, a crackerjack accountant, will see to it that the former occupant doesn't fall into arrears. We'll make sure he sends his old mom, the only personal correspondent we could determine, a Christmas card.

We razed the rampant growth on the property. The children have resumed playing in the trucks, and we've accepted that boys will be boys. The little Jesus fish on the Dodge Ram has sprouted rudimentary legs and a tail, clearly one of Stefan's jokes, although he denies it. It's so peaceful here on our cul-de-sac, at the edge of the ravine, that it's difficult to recall that only two months ago we were engaged in what Patel has described as a Manichean struggle.

The smell is something we've learned to live with, even Trevor. A kind of sufferance we must bear.

Looking out our front windows we can see our wives, curbside, straddling their motorcycles, careful of their gently swelling bellies, revving their engines. The flash of late-October sun on chrome fenders, after all the rain we've had lately, could render a man blind.

ONCE, WE WERE SWEDES

No one cared about the facts anymore. The facts were suspect, mutable as memory, as insubstantial as the off-gassing of the new polymer carpets in the classroom, their molecular composition resistant to the most persistent of stains: mustard, cherry Kool-Aid, blood. (Alex's students had all shrugged when she asked if anyone else could smell the fumes that insinuated their way into her sinus cavities and then slumped there like a belligerent toddler, half-dressed and shrieking.)

As for news, baby, these kids wouldn't notice news if it kicked down their doors in the dull of the night and set their hair on fire.

What they had were opinions. And in their opinion Journalism 100 badly sucked. Where was the *equipment*? Where were the DVCPRO digital camcorders, the Avid XP editing suite, the chroma wall for weather, the skyline backdrop? And why do research for news stories when you could blog or tweet what you already knew? That the two "newsroom" printers were dot matrix was cause for much hilarity. The archetypical steno pad and rollerball pen, iconic to Alex, might as well have been the mandible fragments of an iguanodon.

Who were they, these wounded children of the new diaspora with their burnt offerings of exploding car radiators and near rapes in strip-mall ATM lobbies as excuses? Who was forcing them to be here? One sallow boy with gaping nostrils had shown up last month, assignment incomplete as usual, his right hand swathed in gauze like a badly applied diaper. He held it up as if taking a citizenship oath, claiming second-degree burns. Three days later, Alex caught that same hand, unscathed save for its tattooed knuckles, giving her the finger as she wrote, yet again, on the whiteboard: *Who, What, Where, When, and Why?*

What she should have written: *Why bother?*

She tried to channel empathy—these were kids whose older brothers were being gunned down gangland-style in the driveways of their parents' suburban strongholds, whose older sisters were engaged to men they'd never met from countries they'd never been to. She saw them gathered around the entrance to the Terry Fox SkyTrain station like rejects from a casting call for a movie set in South Central L.A. The girls were almost beautiful when viewed from a distance and not under simmering compact fluorescents, their hair a startling platinum or copper-green against caramel skin; the one pallid girl's hair a fretful black. Waiting there for whatever it was they felt the world owed them.

Corinna D. had yet to finish an assignment. She stood planted regally in front of Alex, empty-handed, her eggshell eyelids at half-mast. Statuesque, petulant, she spoke with a liquid West Indies accent although born in Ladner, and wrote English as if it were a second, or even third, language. Most of them wrote it this way, but Corinna with particular finesse. ("In my own onion this Teecher have no Peoples skills," she would write on her class evaluation. And the Teecher would attempt a snort of laughter while reading this alone on her front stoop as she watched the dispossessed drifting through the aborted heritage renovation across the street.)

Corinna tugged out her earbuds. "So, I was clubbing with my cousins." Every anecdote of Corinna's began with her cousins—whether blood relations or a code word for something else, Alex had never figured out. Corinna's story involved a drive along No. 5 Road, hitting something, Cousin Kevin arguing with Cousin Tristan about whether to stop or not. What looked like blood-smeared blond hairs on one of the tires. Cousin Kendra screaming that she just wants to get the fuck home ("That girl has the mouth in the family"). A lumpy green garbage bag in the middle of the road. More arguing along with the requisite *Fuck you*s between Kevin and Tristan about who was going to look in the bag.

"And I'm all, I'm checking out the bag already." Corinna sighed heavily and actually looked right at Alex—a first—as if to say, *Men*. She pulled a strand of gum from her mouth, rolled it into a little green ball. "You do *not* wanna know."

The garbage bags with their grisly contents had started appearing in the fall and had by now become the stuff of urban legend around Vancouver. Everyone claimed to know someone who knew someone who knew someone who had stumbled across one, always at night, always somewhere near water, but the authorities were keeping it quiet. No one had even been reported missing.

Alex waved her hand towards the classroom door with what she thought was a coolly comic flourish and said, "Creative Writing, Room 209, Block D." No one laughed except for the enormous congenial boy at the back of the room whose real name, as far as Alex could discern from class records, was Xmas Singh. She called him X and he pulled in solid Bs and feigned amusement at her jokes. You took what you could get.

Here in Room 017, Block C, in the bowels of one of those community colleges proliferating bunny-like on the outskirts of the metropolis, cheek-to-rump with industrial pig farms, ginseng plantations, and warehouse outlets, sarcasm might as well have been an advanced form of skin disease. She used to be so good with words. Now, more often than not, Alex found herself at a loss. There was a time when she had been fluent in more than one language. Alex and Rufus used to speak IKEA with each other, a language redolent with umlauts and nursery-rhyme rhythms. *Drömma. Blinka. Sultan Blunda!* It was lingonberry of another tongue—tart, sexy even, in a birch-veneer kind of way. Their private lingua franca.

While the rest of the class fiddled with their iPods and iPhones, Corinna D. drifted towards a workstation as if walking the red carpet, plopped down, and swivelled her chair around, thumbs already busy texting one of her cousins.

It was the year provincial health insurance had started covering Botox injections and teeth-whitening technology for the disenfranchised. Thirty-three-year-old female heroin addicts who had appeared sixty now looked like ageless *Fireball XL5* puppet people. They jittered around expressionless, eyes wide, their remaining teeth gleaming like Chiclets between pillowy Jolie Lips™.

Buildings were crumbling; major developments sat abandoned, skeletal. Steel girders pointed skyward with nothing cloaking them, but the people who squatted amongst them looked defiantly better. This was the new harm reduction.

The Atlanta-based *Journal for the Society of Aesthetic Medicine* published a study confirming that positive self-image was the first step towards recovery and self-reliance.

It wasn't only the prematurely aged homeless who were looking younger. A candidate for mayor was shown on the news playing beach volleyball. Her face was drum-tight, and saucy pigtails sprouted from the sides of her head, but her cellulite-buckled butt cheeks, split by a thong, looked like navel oranges in a sling.

She had a good serve, though, the anchor and the weatherman agreed, *a damn fine serve.*

Alex, who used to report on insurgents in Chad and Sudan, was perched at her breakfast bar, two weeks' worth of newspapers and flyers towering at her elbows, spying on a student after hours. She was surprised to find the name of the lawyer Corinna D. had said Cousin Kevin had called—even before he called the police about the body—right there in the phone book, between Wells Fargo Financial and Wells, Jocelyn, aromatherapy. Her chest felt unaccountably bound as she pressed the numbers, as if she were lying abandoned in a play dungeon in second-hand fetish gear. She who had interviewed a leader of the Janjaweed in Darfur and not broken a sweat. She had felt not so much fear then, but anger. And bewilderment.

"I know the party in question," the lawyer informed Alex, but wouldn't—couldn't—disclose anything more.

She told him: "You have to understand; I'm just doing my job."

It sounded feeble, even to her. What was she now, some low-level SS officer?

The stink from the classroom carpet was still lodged in her nostrils. That, and the smell of something altogether worse, thumbprinted in memory from a distance of some years and many miles.

Alex and Rufus were combing through the takeout pad thai for the remaining shrimp bits when she told him she wanted to quit the college. It didn't pay that well, anyway. The commute, from Broadway station to Terry Fox, was like spending time in medium security. The industrial carpets were rendering her cataleptic. And there was a moral malaise spreading fungus-like among the students that she feared might be contagious.

"Fungal strife." Rufus laughed. "The jock itch of the soul."

"It's not even that they're hard." She wanted him to take this seriously. "Hard is at least some kind of position. It's more like they're—squishy." She didn't mention the body in the garbage bag and her call to the lawyer.

Rufus pointed his chopsticks at her. "Lex, do you think maybe you've forgotten what it's like to be a kid?" She was thirty-six; he was six years older but was intent on pretending he hadn't yet turned forty. He'd recently taken to scootering to work on a collapsible Razor that he could sling across his back in its own little carrying case. He wore a Tyrolean felt hat that had belonged to his Austrian grandfather, but it might as well have been a little striped beanie with a plastic propeller on top. It served her right, she thought, for marrying a man named for a beloved family pet.

They had been together for seven years, and had been living in the duplex on Venables for five now, married. Rufus's dry wit used to be like kindling stacked around her heart. It was in the giddy days of moving in together that IKEA talk had been born. As he flopped onto the new mattress, Rufus had beckoned, "Join me in *Sultan Blunda*, a cloud forest of cheap vodka, Astrid Lindgren characters, and common sense." Now when Alex lay down on the bed, sometimes in the middle of the day, it no longer felt like *Sultan Blunda*; it felt like a mattress that had gone flat and lumpy. A sad blunder.

When had they stopped talking IKEA? When she inherited that Ethan Allen–style credenza from her mother last summer, her first *real* piece of furniture, while Rufus had slapped together shelves made of plastic milk crates and two-by-fours in the basement to hold his growing new/old collection of vinyl from stores like Zulu and Red Cat? Places where middle-aged men in black concert T-shirts shot the shit with concave-chested kids who had rogue chin hairs and opinions about everything from whether Muse frontman Matt Bellamy was really the late Jeff Buckley with plastic surgery to the latest conspiracy theory about the government monitoring all Internet use in collusion with an online ad conglomerate. Or was it before that, when she came back from Africa for the last time and tried to convince herself that those who could no longer *do* could teach?

Rufus was looking at her too intently, his chopsticks noodling in the air as if painting a devil's Vandyke on her face.

"What?" she said, flicking at the corners of her mouth with her fingers, thinking maybe a bean sprout slick with peanut oil was hanging there maggot-like. "What?"

"Do you ever get the feeling we're too white?"

His new code word for too old. Did he mean *she* was too white?

"*Smila Blomma*," Alex said, aiming for playfulness, hoping for some esprit de corps. "*Fira, Slabang.*"

The words floated in the air like cat dander for what seemed like several very long dead seconds. Rufus finally smiled indulgently. "*SKÄRPT!*"

Skärpt like a knife. *Skärpt* like a machete.

Was Rufus being deliberately mean or—worse—had he forgotten?

It was the year of the endless civic election. Campaign signage was everywhere, but this was indicative less of the spirit of democracy than of a sense of desperation. A new municipal bylaw allowed citizens to accept payment to display signs and billboards. You could tell when someone was really hard up when ads for Farsighted People and the Fiscally Responsible Folks and Greener than You, plus various independents, all jostled for space on the same patchy scrap of front lawn. The lawns of the kind of people who donated sperm to fertility clinics at $50 a pop and dreamt of selling a kidney on eBay. It was hard to pass judgment; these weren't easy times.

Sustainability Is for Suckers, an FRF slogan read. The Tim Hortons on Kingsway had it printed on their coffee-cup sleeves. The Kamper Kids wore the discards as armbands. After all, everyone had a right to an opinion.

Alex told her students to write up Corinna's incident on No. 5 Road in inverted-pyramid style for the following week.

She said: You can interview Corinna—she's a *primary source*. She's a *witness*.

She said: Remember to write it with the most important information near the top so that an editor can cut from the bottom up.

She said: Bottoms up, get it?

Xmas Singh said: Hahaha.

She said (to herself): Bonus points for using actual facts.

Not so long ago Rufus used to talk to Alex, really talk, about just about everything, as he sat on the toilet, bathroom door ajar so they could hear each other, peeing for what seemed to her an inordinately long time. A feeble trickle like early-spring melt off a mountain stream. She'd urged him to get his aging prostate checked, fearing the small chestnut gland would start ballooning with tumours bagpipe-like throughout his groin.

Mostly Rufus had talked about his designs. He'd launched a small company with a friend a decade ago that specialized in sustainable designs rooted in the natural world. "Bionical creative engineering," Rufus called it. He'd won a Suzuki Foundation Award for developing a non-toxic fabric finish inspired by water-repellent lotus leaves. More recently he'd been obsessively studying the mako shark and its *hydrodynamic proportions*, its enviable *zero-friction drag*. A superhero shark. Nature's Genius—Human/e Technology (the name had been Alex's idea) was in negotiations with a Miami-based underwater-exploration outfit to underwrite the clean technology Rufus was developing.

Alex lowered the newspaper after rereading the same sentence about the doomed Inga Falls hydroelectric project on the Congo River at least five times. (Kimberly Lum never could write a lead.) "So what does Ernesto Jr. say about your latest mako calculations?" The millionaire Cuban American had started lowballing Rufus on materials almost from the word go.

Rufus, hunched over his laptop at the coffee table, the can of Red Bull at his elbow replacing his usual green tea, glanced at her briefly and shrugged. "It's complicated." He turned back to *World of Warcraft: Final Blood*. This guy who hadn't even heard of *Tetris* when she met him had somehow, while she wasn't looking, morphed into a gamer. He belonged to a dejected, renegade race of *draenei*, the Broken. Alex leaned over his shoulders and tried to make sense of the mayhem on his monitor. "So, your guys, are they good guys or bad guys?"

Rufus just rolled his eyes. "It doesn't work like that."

Was it a trick of the light, or was that peach fuzz on his cheeks?

Alex missed her bionical man, as she used to call him, poking a finger into his softening gut. She missed their toilet conversations, the intimacy and vulnerability of a peeing man seated and talking earnestly about his aspirations.

Now, he often stood, aiming from the bathroom doorway in a jet stream. Singing off-key as he whizzed. He seemed happy.

Two of these things were facts. One was just her opinion.

NIGHT ON TOWN TRASHED
By Xmas Singh

Corinna D. and her cousins were just trying to have a good time.

They gone to see dj Jaspa at Viva.

"It was happening," Miss D. said. She was wearing her new lickwid tights.

But some jerk left a pile of garbage in the middle of the road that turned out to be a dead body.
^ allegedly
"Cousin Kevin was pissed," said Miss D. "He just washed that car."

The vehicle was a 2011 Mahindra Scorpio, "a kind of sick green," according to a source.

None of the passengers was injured during the incident.

Richmond police were totally rude when asked for an interview.

-30-

Alex's other students gave no indication that they thought Corinna's story was news.

Her neighbourhood was changing so rapidly that if Alex stood without moving on the corner of East 1st and Commercial Drive, she would find herself at the still centre of a kaleidoscopic time-lapse movie. This is what her neighbourhood had become, a tone poem set to a Philip Glass soundtrack, punctuated with sirens, and drumbeats, and guttural shouts as the local unmedicated or overmedicated argued with themselves and each other while they ranged back and forth across the Drive, dodging cars, bikes, and elderly Italian and Portuguese Canadian jaywalkers.

After a period of intense gentrification, a mini baby boom, and the opening of three overpriced florists and a string of restaurants with beer fresh sheets, there was a sense of emptying out. Her friends who feared the Kamper Kids, the garbage-bag rumours, and commercial rezoning that allowed a methadone-dispensing pharmacy to open within two blocks of the community centre/pool/rink/library fled to the suburbs where they had sworn they'd never go. "I'd rather have an infected needle jabbed deep into my right eye," Alex's neighbour Sasha had told her fiercely on more than one occasion. Now Sasha, her pierced labia, wife Marcia, and four-year-old, Destiny, lived in a semi-gated townhouse complex in Port Coquitlam.

Others were going on spiritual pilgrimages to Varanasi or Amankora or joining the circus. In fact, all around the city children were abandoned to aging relatives or the newly minted private kiddie kennels by their thrill-seeking parents. The older children banded together, moving nomad-like from neighbourhood to neighbourhood, performing odd pantomimes for

spare change. *How can we have children? We are children!*
the parents laughed as they formed their human pyramids or
checked their supply of water-purification tablets needed to
survive their third-world spirit quests.

Mainly, though, there was a lot of talk about moving
off-grid. The grid, that matrix of power and telecommu-
nications, heat and light on command, was something Alex
could understand. She had a healthy respect for the grid. Like
IKEA, like steel-cut Scottish oats and cargo pants, the grid
represented common sense. She would cling to the grid with
bloody, tattered fingers if anyone attempted to dislodge her.
Alex overheard a couple in JJ Bean loudly debating the pros
and cons of a $25,000 residential wind turbine or a bicycle-
powered generator. The woman seemed particularly concerned
about not losing access to Netflix. "If you want to get off the
grid," Alex found herself saying, as if offering advice on the
daily blend, "try sub-Saharan Africa." The woman called her
a racist, Trotskyite bitch. The guy just winked and tongued the
foam on his coffee.

Steel girders formed the roof of the heritage building across
the street—an abandoned Free Methodist church turned
award-winning performance space—replacing the rotting
wood beams of the original. Piece by piece, what was meant
to be a renovation had been slowly turning into a replica, like
those museum reproductions of Bastet cat goddesses and busts
of Pericles you could use for bookends. Now it stood neglected,
the skeleton of some great beast washed ashore on a remote
island and bleached to a pewter gleam by the sun.

And there was Alex with her free-floating sense of hollowness
in her own rib cage. Her period hadn't shown up for over six
weeks, and her first thought was stress, then malignant carpet
fibres. A single polymer thread clinging to her uterus, gathering

her blood and tissue to it, a teething fibrous leech. She waited another week before even contemplating the alternative.

A child? It seemed she already had a child. A playmate for Rufus? There was an idea! Alex found she wasn't as horrified at the thought as she thought she'd be. It could be *Duktig*!

But the stick stayed white. No thin blue line.

Rufus asked: Do you ever wonder if we're too straight? Too fluoridated? Too hydrated?

From: <adinesen@globeandmail.ca>
To: <rufus@bioman.ca>
Sent: February 10, 2008
Subject: ??

Hey Roof? You know the Janjaweed? They call them demons on horseback. There's a guy here, ostensibly with Human Rights Watch, but he has some kind of "deep intelligence" (read: he has something they want). The word is that the Sudanese govt. is backing this raging Arab militia. It's genocide plain and simple. So I get this interview with a demon "general"—this alleged war criminal who arrives at the rendezvous somewhere near his garrison on a camel. And the thing he wants to talk about is dental hygiene. He got his teeth fixed by a recruit who was a dentist in Dubai. Now he religiously uses whitening strips. "Like Hollywood," he tells me. He's supposed to hate the infidels, right? So I stand there dumb as a moth in my chador (de rigueur due to his Muslim sensitivities) while he asks about my dental plan and whether I prefer Crest or Colgate.

This is so hysterically not what I expected that my questions, all the anger that I've been stoking since I got here, go AWOL. And all this time he's leaning in close, flashing these teeth like he's a game-show host, and then he asks to see mine.

It's just him, his camel, and me—and a circle of his men on their horses eyeing us from a distance. My "translator" has wandered off to take a piss. I lift my shroud flap up over my eyes and he makes this sound in his throat, almost like poor old Knob-Goblin's purr used to sound when we snurffled her belly, and puts his finger, which smells like smoke and blood and goat, right into my mouth. He runs it back and forth and back and forth, from molar to molar, while muttering something I take to be, "Nice, nice." I think, I do actually think this, I could bite his finger right off right now, bite down as hard as I can, trapping his filthy child-raping finger and then spitting it out at his feet.

He just keeps running his finger back and forth and so help me god I start to get hot and almost come right there standing in the dry wind stink of him.

What does this make me?? And this whole time I'm in my chador like some black ghost. How can I even tell you this? How can I not?

These are the things we do when we're no longer ourselves. When the self disappears. The self—dear Knob-Goblin, I'd almost forgotten about her.

<delete>

The clinic doctor walked in, tapping a pen against her teeth. She looked about twelve. There was a polished bone (quail? ferret? human fetus?) protruding through both sides of her nostrils, and starting at the top of her hands and scrolling up under the sleeves of her lab coat, some tattooed script, "μνυμι πόλλωνα ητρ ν, κα σκληπι ν, κα γείαν, κα Πανάκειαν, κα θεο ς πάντας τε κα πάσας . . ."

Alex, perched on the examining table in her crackling blue-paper wrapper, had the urge to ID the doctor before she let her slip her child-size hand inside her. She wondered if the girl had even gotten her period yet. Maybe it was bring-your-kid-to-work week? Her own GP, a wiry-haired woman she loved who had seen her through a devastating bout of post-traumatic stress disorder, was away on a Doctors Without Borders mission in Haiti.

Alex stared at the girl doctor's hands to avoid looking directly into her face. "The Hippocratic oath," the doctor said, pulling up her T-shirt to reveal more of the script spiralling across her taut belly. "In the original Greek." Tugging her shirt back into place, she asked Alex a stream of straightforward questions, then snapped on a pair of green-and-white latex gloves embossed with the Starbucks logo, the mermaid with her tail split at her crotch. "We'll have to run a few tests to make sure, but if I'm going to hazard, like, an educated guess? I would say premature ovarian failure."

"What?"

"Early menopause."

Alex heard herself shrieking. The sound of the big ginger tom next door happening upon a raccoon clan in the back alley. Jamie Lee Curtis in *Halloween*. A B-movie screech in Dolby Digital 5.1. On the wall behind the child doctor was a calendar featuring anthropomorphized bacteria engaged in Winter Olympic–style sporting events with an assortment of antibiotic soaps.

"It happens," she told Alex matter-of-factly. To who— whom? To *whom* does this happen at thirty-six?!

Walking home from the clinic, clutching a referral for a geriatrics specialist and a pamphlet on the pros and cons of estrogen replacement therapy, Alex felt the elasticity in her skin giving way with each step, her uterus a dried gourd inside her, rattling like a maraca. She spotted a guy who looked like Rufus putting up a poster on a telephone pole outside Dream Cycle. Staple gun in hand, he scootered up Commercial from pole to pole. That goofy hat, the orange hoodie. It *was* Rufus.

The poster read: *Shuffering Shuccotash at the Iberian Club, Wed. April 13th.* It had a picture of Sylvester the Cat as St. Sebastian, pierced from cartoon ears to foot-paws with arrows. Tweety Bird fluttered above his head with a shit-eating grin and a bow in his fist. A creepy cupid. A malevolent angel.

It was the year of the Benevolent Municipal Bylaw (section iii, clause 8d) that allowed the homeless to camp out in construction sites as long as they signed a personal-injuries waiver. Developers didn't like it, but since the 2010 Olympics and the overextension of credit and enormous cost overruns, sites sat empty. A waste, the majority Farsighted People councillors decided. The opposition FRF agreed, but had wanted to charge rent.

Across the street from Alex's house, under the rib-like girders and jutting rebar, a troupe of Kamper Kids slept each night in a tangled mound like buttered noodles, the remaining stained-glass window casting a fractured mosaic over them whenever the street light came on and flickered through it. During the day they moved on, forming their silent, almost biblical tableaux outside the off-sales, loonie stores, and coffee bars all along Commercial Drive. At dusk they drifted back, lit a small fire, and sat companionably around it passing containers of takeout back and forth until the flames extinguished themselves. And then they slept again.

From: <adinesen@globeandmail.ca>
To: <rufus@bioman.ca>
Sent: February 10, 2008
Subject: way2go!!

Congratulations on your award!! That's *Mammut*, baby.

You're a green machine, Roof.

Same-same here. Hot, heartbreaking—jaded professionals, desperate people. My fingers feel like molten lead just typing about it. Latest in tomorrow's paper. Maybe already online. Sudan still denying it's backing the rampaging Islamic rebels.

Don't worry so much, the Human Rights Watch boys are good to me and share their tp & tipples.

forever & ever, Lex

Why couldn't anyone else smell the damn carpet? Alex sat at the front of the classroom pinching the bridge of her nose and ignoring her students. For the past two weeks she'd been letting them do whatever they wanted, waiting to see who would crack first, her or them. There were only nine days left until the end of spring term.

She was playing hangman on the whiteboard with Xmas Singh while the rest of them deployed blue rinse bio bombs and plasma grenades against digital enemies or thumbed away at their PDAs. All jacked into some device, busy and bored. The only truly weird thing about the situation was that most of them still showed up at all, as if attending class was a condition of some kind of day parole. Or maybe they thought this was all there was, maybe they were satisfied that Alex had sunk to their level of expectation. There was no longer any doubt in anyone's mind; she was simply a bad teacher, as opposed to a badass teacher, the kind who could inspire a group of inner-city toughs to excel at calculus or develop a healthy dollop of self-respect. Sidney Poitier's Sir ("I am sick of your foul language, your crude behaviour, and your sluttish manner"—Alex could just imagine the blank stares if she said something like that), Morgan Freeman's "Crazy Joe" Clark, Edward James Olmos's Mr. Escalante. Maybe she *was* too white.

Corinna D. hadn't shown up for almost three weeks. The one call Alex had made to her home had been answered by a tired-sounding woman who said Corinna was out visiting her cousins. The college's privacy rules prevented Alex from mentioning that Corinna had been a no-show for an awfully long time.

Xmas Singh asked: Is there an X?

Alex added a second leg to the stick man dangling from the noose.

Xmas Singh clutched theatrically at his throat and made gurgling noises.

Alex said: Best of three?

Rufus asked: Too settled? Too happy?

"Shuffering Shuccotash?" Alex said, peering at Rufus over the top of her new drugstore reading glasses. They were lying in bed, Rufus shuffling through his latest batch of Pokémon trading cards and Alex squinting at a pamphlet on osteoarthritis.

"My band."

"*Your* band?"

"Our first gig is on the thirteenth."

"But you don't even play an instrument. You're tone-deaf."

"I'm the gear guy."

Her triceps had sagged like saddlebags in the mirror after her bath, her hands ached, her ovaries were shutting down, and this morning she had plucked forty-three more grey hairs from her head before she stopped counting and swept the offending nest into the toilet. When she flushed, the hairs had swirled into a small, furious animal before disappearing with a gurgle. Alex started to cry.

"You're supposed to be the guy making sharkskin so we can all live in the water when the air gets too hot." Alex smacked at Rufus, hard and fast with both hands, like an inspired jazz drummer. "You're supposed to be focusing on saving the planet."

He grabbed her wrists and pulled her towards him, nuzzling her neck. His chest was smoother than when she'd met him, the curve of his penis like a scimitar. He smelled hairless, like peeled cantaloupe.

"I can't do this anymore," Alex muttered. "It's starting to feel like incest."

But she closed her eyes and rose to try to meet him halfway.

It was the year the enterprising homeless constructed ad hoc villages of tidy huts from purloined election signs. The colourful little houses lined the cut at both ends of the Terminal Street Bridge. The design world took notice, with the San Francisco–based architectural magazine *Dwell* running a photo essay with text by Toronto's latest public intellectual. "These intelligent spaces represent design that fully integrates the residents' ideals and values with their needs. Like the yurt and the Quonset hut, the 'signage-home' or 'Sigho' will no doubt evolve well beyond its origins, co-opted by those with a discerning eye for the frugality and transportality of the design." He supplied the requisite Walter Benjamin quote from "The Work of Art in the Age of Mechanical Reproduction" and ended with some McLuhanesque wordplay.

Engineered so beautifully they could only have been the work of a down-on-his-luck architect or an idiot savant, the small homes were like snowflakes—no two alike, and yet of a whole. The *Vancouver Sun* ran a contest to find the designer (first prize: a weekend at Sooke House B&B), which led to bewildered bottle ladies and Dumpster divers being ambushed by retired couples waving notebooks and bombarding them with questions about Walter Gropius and deconstructivism and offering a home-cooked meal in exchange for blueprints.

A candidate for mayor declared that she would live for a week in a hut made entirely of her own election signs down among "the people." A newscast ran some unfortunate footage of her crawling out the opening on all fours, tight pigtails pulling her eyes into the coveted pan-Asian look, her breasts visible through her gaping neckline, sagging like sodden pantyhose.

The anchor and weatherman smiled at each other. *Damn fine serve, though*, they reminisced as the sportscaster joined them.

Alex dreamt about a green garbage bag on her front steps. "Happy Birthday, Toots," Rufus says in the dream. And she *is* a Toots, all dolled up in short shorts, pointy cone-shaped black bra, hair pincurled, her lips thick with cherry-scented gloss. She's selling cartons of cigarettes with pictures of missing children on them, big-eyed, black-velvet, paint-by-numbers kids. The bag evidently contains her gift. Rufus grabs her arm as if he can't wait to show her.

Inside the garbage bag Corinna D. stretches languorously and yawns. There are no teeth in her cavernous mouth. Her eyes gleam. *You do not wanna know*, she says. Alex looks from Rufus to Corinna and then jabs her own thumbs right into her eyes. It doesn't hurt a bit.

Onstage, a DJ dressed like a tennis player mixed Harry Belafonte's "Day-O" with something from Trooper. It was early, and the crowd appeared sparse, spread around the barn-like space at tables that looked as if they belonged in a bingo hall. Posters of flamenco dancers, bullfighters, and beaches lined the wood-panelled walls. Beside the bar, which featured Super Bock on tap, Portuguese bean soup, and calamari, there was a framed photograph of a young man with his fist raised, inscribed, "*Camarada! Trabaja y Lucha por la Revolución!*" Rufus handed Alex a foaming pint and steered her towards a small group near the stage. A wiry old man off to the side shadowboxed with what looked in the dim light like a blackened and enormous ham hanging from the ceiling.

The guys in the band were awfully sweet. They clustered around as Rufus introduced her, telling Alex how awesome it was that she had decided to come. She wondered what Rufus had told them about her—that she had terminal cancer or was agoraphobic? The band was Gideon, Attila, and Suki, who was not a guy, but neither was she a threat. She was bald and so skeletal Alex wondered where she'd left her intravenous drip, and wore a Canada Post uniform, the pant cuffs curling under the heels of her shoes, her yellowed, bulging eyes darting about like a cartoon snail's.

They were joined by a kid with a faux-hawk and wearing an oversized hoodie that made his legs look so short he appeared dwarf-like. He slapped Rufus on the shoulder. "Cool, Roof, you brought your mom!"

Alex was beyond her hot flashes by now and their accompanying hormonal riptides or she would have leapt on him like a pit bull and clamped her jaws onto one of his goofy ears. But she appeared to be the only one who had heard. The others were animatedly debating whether to begin or encore with "Tweety's Lament" and whether it would be too clichéd for Attila to do a drum solo. Alex air-kissed in the kid's direction and then ran the tip of her tongue around her lips. The dwarf-boy quickly fled, her past-its-best-before-date sexuality apparently as effective as a bio bomb.

A candidate for mayor shuffled and bobbed between the now crammed tables, dispensing fist bumps as if they were lollipops. "Dissin' the safe injection site—thas wack!" he yelped, while his handlers followed sheepishly at a distance. He was wearing a do-rag, Alex noted, absent-mindedly patting at her thinning scalp. That he was third-generation Chinese Canadian and had gone to school at St. George's on the west side and then Trinity College, U of T, before coming back to Vancouver to start a Pacific Rim polling firm didn't seem strokes against him in this age of reinvention. A camera crew from MuchMusic was following him around, so now this had become an event. There was some giddy talk between Gideon and Rufus about getting on *disBand* and scouts from EMI, and finally Shuffering Shuccotash took the stage to a bunch of raucous *whoot whoots* and whistles.

A girl with an adorable pixie cut atop an Audrey Hepburn neck eyed Rufus as he jumped onstage at the last minute to retape a cable and adjust Gideon's mike—his shoulder blades jutting like nascent wings through his thin T-shirt, his small butt tight in faded jeans. Alex felt a wave of vertigo and had to lean up against the wall. Dangling beside her, the large ham, which she had taken to be synthetic, glistened and gave off whiffs of smoke and fat. The odour of something not so long ago alive, now decidedly dead.

With Gideon on banjo, Attila at the drum kit, and Suki pummelling away at an accordion, they made a noise both discordant and melodic. They were off-kilter but almost great, Alex thought, and judging by the crowd's response, this wasn't just her opinion. And Rufus, was he an almost-great roadie? *Could* you be an almost-great roadie? Dozens surged onto the dance floor, moving in a way that couldn't really be called dancing but was something nonetheless.

In the middle of the melee, there was Xmas Singh shaking it, his bulk surprisingly graceful, like the milky blobs undulating inside a lava lamp, his trademark good-natured smile elevated to something almost beatific. Alex sidled over to him. He didn't look surprised to see her. "Thanks for the B!" He grinned, executing what could be called a pirouette. "I love these guys! They're my gods!"

"But it's just their first gig," Alex yelled above the din. "Isn't it?"

Gideon screamed into his mike: "I tawt I taw a puddy tat!"

The crowd screamed back: "You did, you did, you did taw a puddy tat!"

Isn't it?

Rufus asked: Too *something?*

It was the year a candidate for mayor disappeared from her designer homeless dwelling *into thin air*. Or so it seemed. The double-decker tour buses with the beluga ads on their sides stopped driving by the election-sign shantytown along the Terminal Street Bridge; schools cancelled field trips. Wasn't it only the already invisible or criminally suspect who disappeared *without a trace?* A massive ground search by combined metro police forces and the RCMP came up with zero. Some speculated that the pressure for the mayoralty had become too much and she was recovering on a wind-powered organic vineyard in the Similkameen Valley, pruning vines and smoking weed. Off-grid, so to speak.

When the garbage bags and their grisly contents finally made the news—front-page news, top-of-the-hour news, breaking Internet news—on the local evening TV newscast the anchor and weatherman couldn't meet each other's eyes.

If her students had asked, had they been the least bit curious, Alex could have offered them this fact: In 2009 she saw a machete hack a man's arm right off. Saw this. Someone flashed his white teeth at her and without wiping the blade, strode on. Her own weapons of choice, a spiral notebook and a rollerball pen, useless in her hands.

"Hey, you live 'round here?"

Alex was walking up Commercial towards Santa Barbara

Market, nerves frail as old lace from the club the night before, as if singed by an electrical fire. She couldn't tear her eyes from the totem pole tattoos on the bulging calves of a man who was ambling along ahead of her, skateboard tucked under his arm. The double sets of Raven and Bear eyes had followed her whether she moved left or right. When he stopped to greet someone, Alex recognized the face, framed by long, grey hair, of a native elder she'd interviewed years back at that standoff in Clayoquot Sound. He should have looked ancient, he should've been *dead* by now, he'd been so old at the time (though defiant, lying in front of a John Deere Harvester, passively resisting as the RCMP carried him off), but his face was now smooth and burnished like new copper against his steel locks.

"This your 'hood?" came the voice again. It was Corinna D. But not the Corinna of a month ago. This Corinna, leading two small boys by the hand, was a stout, middle-aged woman, though still regal in bearing. The word *matriarch* sprang to mind, embroidered in cross-stitching, giving off a comforting vibe. The boys were fighting loudly over a Nintendo DS. Corinna wrenched it from them and dangled it above her head while the boys paddled at the air ineffectually.

"This is Cousin Kevin and this is Cousin Tristan," she said, plopping the gaming console into an enormous handbag, and then holding each boy up by a wrist as if offering them for sale. "Boys, say hello to my teacher Ms. Alex Dinesen." Alex was surprised Corinna actually knew her name. Her eyes looked warmer, even welcoming, the lids no longer on sentry duty. Or was that just the difference between seeing someone in daylight versus under fluorescent lights?

"You stopped coming to class," Alex said, not sure what she expected from Corinna at this point. An apology? Absolution? The class, like so much of her life, was now mere historical fact, receding into a mist of could-haves and should-haves. She stroked her crepe-paper neck, a new habit, as she waited for Corinna to reply.

"I can give you some lotion for that," Corinna said, digging around in her bag. She pulled out a small amber-coloured bottle. "You have to shake it real good and then massage it in before bed. It works so well you'd swear it was voodoo." She laughed with her mouth open, teeth all there, shiny and white.

A candidate for mayor strode past, swinging a gold-tipped cane, his white spats gleaming, and tipped his bowler to Corinna. "The Widow D., looking mighty fine. Don't forget to exercise your franchise." Corinna waved him off with a "Shush now." The cousins simultaneously whined, "We're missing *Prank Patrol*/I have to pee!"

A group of Kamper Kids drifted by wearing nubbly oatmeal-shaded robes, like the deeply hooded monks in *A Canticle for Leibowitz*. You could no longer tell the girls from the boys. They stopped a few feet away and began to perform a panto-mime. One of them bent low and put a hand to his (or her?) back, while another stood tall and raised arms above her (or his?) head as if wielding a mighty axe. Several knelt in prayer and a couple of others held out hands, palm over palm, beseech-ingly towards passersby. They froze in tableaux as a siren sliced across East 1st and someone yelled out of an overhead window, "*Armand, do not, I said— Armand!!*"

"I have been young, and *now* am old," Corinna said quietly, "yet have I not seen the righteous forsaken, nor his seed begging bread. Psalms, 37:25."

From the Kamper Kids came a low murmuring that cohered into a chant: "*Nun puer fui siquidem senui et non vidi iustum derelictum neque semen eius quaerens panem.*"

Or vice versa, thought Alex. But that was just her opinion.

For your final exam

Write an editorial piece on the following: Why did the reporter ask for the African assignment? Are witnessed atrocities more real than unwitnessed? (See: "If a tree falls in the forest …" Bishop George Berkeley, philosopher of immaterialism—or the metaphysics of "subjective idealism.") How near the flames can you stand and not get burnt? Take your time before handing in your final draft. Take a lifetime.

N.B. Don't let the facts get in the way of a good story.

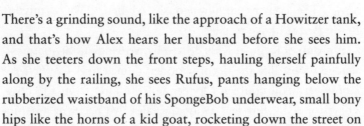

There's a grinding sound, like the approach of a Howitzer tank, and that's how Alex hears her husband before she sees him. As she teeters down the front steps, hauling herself painfully along by the railing, she sees Rufus, pants hanging below the rubberized waistband of his SpongeBob underwear, small bony hips like the horns of a kid goat, rocketing down the street on a skateboard, his feet huge, with their two sideways baby toes that had always made them seem so vulnerable despite their size, inside ratty sneakers, laces flapping.

"I knew a girl in Africa," Rufus once said, back when they still lolled about in *Sultan Blunda*, "and she was the bravest girl in the world."

Well, that was a fact.

I used to love you, she could shout. We used to be happy! Once, we were Swedes!

But even without the green plastic buds in his ears all he would hear was the clacking of her new dentures, large and loose in her mouth.

She could be saying, *Kaxig! Minnen Fackla!*

She could be saying, Tie your shoes, *Besta!*

GLOSSARY

(in order of appearance)—IKEA product in parenthesis:

Drömma	to dream (Lycocel flat sheets)
Blinka	to blink (pillow)
Sultan Blunda	noble man & to shut your eyes (mattress)
Smila Blomma	smiling flower (children's wall lamp – light pink or white)
Fira	celebrate (storage system – mini chest for CDs)
Slabang	funny (alarm clock)
Skarpt	sharp or sharply, suddenly (kitchen knife series and ceramic sharpener)
Duktig	good, well-behaved (toy cookware)
Mammut	mammoth, huge (children's furniture series)
Kaxig	cocky, overconfident (children's pendant lamp – blue or white/green)
Minnen Fackla	memories, reminiscences & a torch (children's wall lamp with flickering "torch light" option)
Besta	asshole, blockhead, doofus (TV storage unit)

FLOATING LIKE A GOAT

Or, What we talk about when we talk about art

Don't let that horse

                        eat that violin

            cried Chagall's mother

                        But he

        kept right on

               painting

And became famous

            —LAWRENCE FERLINGHETTI,
           A CONEY ISLAND OF THE MIND

Dear Miss Subramanium,
    It may strike you as ridiculous (as it did my husband) that
I could lose several nights' sleep over the fact that Georgia

is "not yet meeting expectations" in art. It's *only* art, my husband told me. She's *only* in grade one. But lose sleep I did, and in fact I am now in such a deeply caffeinated fugue state that I fear my letter to you will come across as intemperate. That is not my intent.

Please note that I am not suggesting Georgia is some kind of artistic genius or that she even has any particular talent. This is a defence of artistic expression, not of my daughter's abilities. Or rather, a defence of art itself.

Your penchant for feathered dreamcatcher earrings and tight, sequined T-shirts bearing the names of various headbanger acts has not gone unnoticed among the parents (my husband in particular seems more inclined to pick up our daughter this year than when she was in Mrs. Tam's kindergarten class—where, FYI, Georgia did manage to "fully meet expectations" in art). I take it you may think this gives you a somewhat "free-spirited" or "bohemian" air. But bohemian resides not merely in the costume, Miss Subramanium.

There was a time when I would gladly have sold my soul to curry favour with a particular curatorial demagogue, but I can tell you with certain authority that even back then I would never have stooped to impose strictures on others. A free-spirited woman does not make girls and boys form separate lines before they can enter the classroom, she does not restrict conversation during snack time, and she most certainly does not insist that when six-year-old children draw people or animals their feet MUST be touching the ground.

When my daughter informed me of this "rule," despite the tears of frustration puckering her drawing of our late cat, O'Keeffe, I couldn't suppress a snort. (Not an attractive habit, I admit, and one I'm attempting to rein in after a particularly ill-timed one at the head table of my husband's annual

Conservative Party fundraiser—I blamed the dill sprig on the poached salmon.) "I guess she's never heard of Chagall," I said to Georgia, trying to sound offhand, as I'm well aware that it's considered verboten to undermine a teacher's authority. Georgia, ever curious, wanted to know more, so I hauled out my dusty Gardner's *Art Through the Ages*, only to find that the small black-and-white photograph of *The Crucifixion* did little to convey the intensity of vision and colour and the infectious joie de vivre of Chagall's work. The Internet proved a more satisfying resource, as it frequently does these days.

Georgia was most taken with the goats—floating, soaring, violin-playing goats. "I wish I could fly," she said, more pensively than her tender age warrants. Well, who doesn't? (Do you suppose we could purchase posters of *La baie des Anges* for only $56.01 plus shipping or a boxed set of eight Chagall greeting cards online today if daydreamy little Marc Chagall had been in *your* grade one class, Miss Subramanium? Just a thought.)

I am an actuary by trade. My job involves evaluating risk. This has been ranked the number one low-stress occupation in the country, according to recent media reports, and I can attest to their veracity (which is why my dentist finds it so surprising that I grind my teeth in the night—bruxism, it's called. That sounds like the name of an art movement, does it not? Something darkly male, something tantalizingly *unkempt*. My No. 14 and No. 19 molars have evidently suffered such irreparable damage that it threatens to alter the appearance of my jawline. I'm currently awaiting delivery of my custom-fitted mouthguard, my own *nocturnal bite plate*. This is the kind of excitement I have to look forward to these days, Miss Subramanium).

As both a professional and a parent, it is my job to

calculate risks, not take them. Taking risks—that is the
artist's, and the child's, job.

Your feet-on-the-ground dictum, or "rool," as Georgia put
it in her journal, is just the starting point. There is also your
oft-stated desire that the children make their crayon strokes in
one direction and one direction only, putting cross-hatching
on the same criminal level as giving a classmate a wedgie. And
snipping the erasers off the ends of their pencils so that they're
forced to confront their "mistakes"—I won't even go there
right now. What I would like to focus on is your insistence
that a drawing is not complete until the child has filled in the
background.

Can I call your attention to the Toronto painter Ronald
Bloore? Most famous for his white-on-white paintings of the
1970s and '80s, which he has said represent "freedom for the
viewer," Bloore is a master of texture. The aesthetic pleasure
of these works lies in the very white space you claim to abhor.
The intra-textural space *is* the image. (I came so close to buying
a Bloore once at auction, but my husband, much like you,
Miss Subramanium, could not see the value in the pristine
expansiveness of the painting, calling it—I'm almost embarrassed to type the phrase lest you think he speaks like this in
front of Georgia—"a wank job." It could be that my husband
was jealous. If you have seen photographs of Bloore in his
middle years you would agree that he had a rakish quality, that
airborne charisma of the rogue male artist confident in his abilities and able to draw people, namely women, effortlessly into
his vortex. He is, at that age, a doppelgänger for my dentist.
The resemblance is rather uncanny, save that my dentist does
not dangle a cigarette between his fingers as he plies his trade.)

To focus so intently on the absence of colour. To trust
the viewer to distinguish between different kinds of

whiteness—between *degrees* of whiteness. There is a bold
erotic charge to this deliberate withholding. Bloore himself
once called art "a three-letter word." Can you understand the
rigour involved in denial, Miss Subramanium?

This is not to say that a child handing in a blank sheet of
paper and calling it art should be met with cries of *bravis-
simo!* (although it would be rather clever), but that art is
elastic and your insistence on mimetic drawings, complete
with backgrounds, rather retrograde.

I can almost hear you sighing, Miss Subramanium. It isn't
my tendency to psychoanalyze, but it's not difficult to imagine
what this fear of white space implies. You don't like to be
alone, do you? Whiling away empty hours fills you with an
unnameable terror, does it not? There are people who can help
with this—God knows I have a list of contacts as long as my
arm. Just say the word.

The point of art, Miss Subramanium, is in *not* meeting
expectations. Ha! Yes, that is the point! I surprise even myself
with this revelation. So Georgia, in "not yet meeting expectations," is, in fact, at the top of her class. Art, and here I
include dance, music, film, and belles lettres, is perhaps the
only human activity where not meeting expectations corre-
sponds with success, not failure.

And in a life full of almost continual, albeit inconsequen-
tial, disappointments, with others, with ourselves, in a life full
of notable *failure* (to secure a date with Daryl Sawatsky for
the high-school graduation dance; to place in the top percen-
tile of your statistics class despite pulling enough all-nighters
and popping enough bennies to fell an aurochs), this ability
of the few to defy, to subvert, expectations gives the rest of
us something to live for—vicariously, in the third person as it
were.

In all fairness I should tell you that your self-referential habit when addressing the children has become a source of amusement at our house. Miss S. is getting frustrated over the level of the noise in the classroom. Miss S. needs someone to run to the office and get her some Tylenol 3s. Miss S. needs a minute to finish her text message to her ex-boyfriend. "Miss S. sounds likes Dobbie in *Harry Potter*," Georgia said the other day, and we shared a laugh, picturing you as the beleaguered house elf smashing yourself on the head with a desk lamp after one transgression or another. That actually brought some tears to my eyes. (My husband came to your defence; feathered earrings and patchouli-scented heavy-metal cotton Ts no doubt dangling like sugarplums over his head.)

Perhaps you come from a troubled home or even a troubled country, if your last name is any indication. It is not in my nature to pry. But your quest for order appears to me a manifestation of an obsessive need to wield complete control over your small fiefdom. The word *martinet* comes to mind. How am I as a parent to know that an ill-timed scrawl outside the lines won't trigger a psychotic episode due to undiagnosed post-traumatic stress disorder; that you're not above administering medieval forms of punishment? How am I to ascertain that my child is safe in your classroom, with its almost Pol Pot-ish rules about behaviour? What's next, Miss Subramanium, a pile of polished skulls in the supply cupboard?

Can I call you Shayana, Miss Subramanium? Miss Subramanium is, after all, a mouthful, and so formal considering I am technically old enough to be your mother. As for Miss S.—well, I'm hardly one of your little charges.

There was a time, Shayana, when I wore my era's equivalent to your dreamcatchers and rebellious T-shirts. I had aspirations. I was giddy with my own sexual power—a simulacrum of power fed by the illusions of youth and a type of wan beauty, but power of a kind nonetheless. Every day brought a new opportunity for adventure. Did I imagine then that I would spend the bulk of my days, year upon year, in a small office cubicle with an Excel spreadsheet on the monitor in front of me, a photograph of a laughing girl on a portable potty as my screen saver, and on my desk a miniature inflatable punching bag (a Secret Santa gift from my colleagues) of the existential figure from Munch's *The Scream*? Not for a moment. I was going to be an artist.

I had an advantage over my fellow students at the art college—I could see voices as colours and shapes, and without the aid of any psychotropic. As long as someone was talking, I had a palette to work with. The nasal Upper Canada monotone of my life-class instructor produced oddly compelling anorexic oatmeal-streaked buttocks and breasts (you may imagine how this annoyed the model, who was rather voluptuous and rosy hued, but the sketches earned me instant recognition as an iconoclast). My roommate's throaty smoker's laugh gave me a series of large canvas magma flares in reds, oranges, and basalt. The melancholy-flecked sound of my Estonian landlady talking to her daughter over the telephone, a small umbral gem.

Recorded voices, digitized voices, mediated voices didn't have any effect. This synesthesia only worked "live." Walking along a crowded street was quite literally a psychedelic experience. "Your voice is damaged swimwear," I told a stranger waiting for a bus, a pimply-faced teen whose girlfriend poked him in the ribs with her pointy little elbow before he could respond. "You sound like fresh cement," I said to a waitress midway through her recitation of the daily specials.

I was flying, that's what it felt like. Until the day I came across a man whose voice I couldn't see.

Have you ever had a demon lover, Shayana?

Forget bad-boy musicians or beautiful vampires. I'm talking about the kind of man who turns his dirty dishes over and, when both sides are used, throws them out in a way that is both ceremonial and completely nonchalant, and has you utterly, utterly convinced that this is a "philosophy." A man who adds not one but three umlauts to his name for a devastating Teutonic effect. I'm talking about a terrifying and destructive charisma.

He was famous for a time, and then infamous. This was the mid-eighties, when money flowed towards the neo-expressionists like blood from an unstanched head wound. Basquiat. Fischl. Salle. Schnabel. He was the unacknowledged leader of the neo-geo movement, a concerted assault on the neo-expressionists, whom he deemed hopeless—and dangerous—Romantics. (A danger to art, that is.) You may have come across his name somewhere recently because of the unresolved court case, in a *Vanity Fair* or an *Interview* (although your periodical tastes may run more towards *Us* and *Hello!*—to each his or her own, I always say). There is a Facebook group, Mephisto's Muses, devoted to his memory. (I'll leave you to judge for yourself the degree of collective self-absorption involved there.) Did he have a disarming grimace? I honestly can't remember.

I'm going to tell you a story, Shayana, and don't be alarmed if it doesn't immediately make sense. Good stories seldom do.

Once upon a time a young woman encountered a man. It doesn't matter how they met. One moment she was up in the air, the next she was falling to earth but didn't care. The man

was not what anyone would call handsome or young. His hair
was stiff and matted, his belly soft, his breath sulphuric; his
eyes had slits for pupils, like a goat's. But when he spoke, all
she could see and hear was his voice. She could *feel* his voice,
she knew she could find him anywhere through echolocation.
It was as if she had become a bat. A small, needy fruit bat.

He said her name often, and every time he did so it was as
if he were pinning her to a corkboard, each pronouncement
of her name a kind of claiming. Why did he want her so? This
went on for some time, this living blind in a cave with only his
voice for company, seldom venturing out in human form.

Near the end of that honeymoon period, they were in
someone's basement den after a long night of flitting from club
to club. How he loved the clubs! The body heat, the insistent
beats, the obliteration of the senses, the fawning recognition
of slinky creatures. The light above the billiard table was
bothering his eyes. Unscrew the bulb, he told her. And she did,
with her bare fingers, barely flinching while onlookers caught
their breath. By this time he had formed a habit of patting
her on the head when she did something that pleased him,
as if she were a loyal pooch, no longer stroking her mouse-
brown fur, her leathered wingtips, no longer content to stay
in their cave. He was spending more and more time with a
woman who kept a steppe wolf in her laundry room. The wolf
mistress, she realized, even then, was the kind of woman she
could never be.

I can grant you any wish you want, he told her that night
she burnt her fingertips. Did he actually say this or only imply
it? Had she invoked him, her demon, like Theophilus or
Faustus, or even poor Robert Johnson down at the crossroad?
She had been content living blind, eating fermenting plums,
breathing deep, the world just brief flickering shadows on the

moist walls of a cave when he lit his bong. What was left that she could wish for?

To be an artist or to be a muse—that was what tore her in two. The spell she was under led her to believe being his muse would be the more fulfilling of the two. And they lived happily ever after. Or so it would seem, for a time.

So you see, thwarted artists can be anywhere, Shayana. There is artistry to Georgia's rages, to my husband's carefully culti- vated philistinism, even to your straining T-shirts with their incoherent stage heroes and faux satanic symbols. There is an artistry to how my dentist scales my bicuspids (yes, he does his own scaling). And when he talks to me, sticking to strictly technical terms as he cups my collapsing jaw in his smooth nitrile-glove-cloaked hand, I can almost hear colours again. (I think he could help you with your overbite, I really do. I am willing to do this, to *share*. You only have to say the word.) My umbral masterpiece hangs above the bidet, to my husband's discomfort, a reminder of how much has been lost and how much has been gained, and of the almost incalcu- lable distance between the two things.

Just let me ask you this, Shayana. Can we honestly say any of us really have our feet firmly on the ground?

Sincerely,

Anne (Georgia's mother)

INVESTMENT
RESULTS MAY VARY

Dan and Patricia O'Donnell are always searching for the best of everything. Here they are now. Patricia—her long, dark hair tied back in an impossibly sleek braid, hair pulled so tight her eyebrows look as if they're about to boomerang around the room—partially reclines on what appears to be a chaise longue. Dan leans against an old-fashioned radiator by an open window, one loafer-clad foot crossed in front of the other, looking like one of those guys in high school Nina always wanted to hump on the leg like a crazed standard poodle. You know, dry-humping away, knees locked, eyes bulging, just to get that self-satisfied smirk off his face. Dan and Patricia's teeth are preternaturally white, boraxed incisors gleaming. Their ceiling soars above them at least sixteen feet. A crudely painted saddle—a swollen lily, Georgia O'Keeffe–inspired, over the seat—vies for wall space with pressed-tin skeletons dangling on wires. The single orchid in an intentionally crooked raku vase on the edge of a spotless glass table screams wabi-sabi pretensions with twice-weekly maid service.

And the light. The light in the room is fantastic. Vermeer, all business, hands on his hips, directing the sun. Of course, there's the berber rug. Not a Paul-Bowles-got-wasted-on-this-rug berber, but creamy, white wool, Yaletown berber.

Nina, sitting cross-legged on her basement suite's futon couch, fennel tea cooling beside her on the upturned milk crate draped with a beach towel, really does want to hate them. She has already started that ascent to the dizzying heights a decent bout of righteous anger can transport her to—that place where the air thins, the blood grows hypoxic, and you can muse on your own demise in an oddly detached manner—but the fine print gets in the way. *Dramatization*, it reads in tiny type at the bottom of the magazine ad. *The clients' names and story are fictitious and intended to be an illustration of services available through Merrill Lynch. Investment results may vary.*

Still, there's that light and the unnerving placement of naïf *objets d'art*. And Patricia, coiled to spring even in repose. It's as if Jeff Wall has done an ad for Merrill Lynch. The People You Will Never Be So Kill Yourself Now (cibachrome, 2006).

Another house on the North Shore has been swallowed by the mountainside. A stunning cliff-edge post-and-beam completed in 1956. It's been happening with alarming frequency lately. There are those who find these disappearances—what else to call them?—less dramatic but more frightening than the mudslides triggered by torrential rains that have destroyed both houses and their inhabitants. Those incidents could be ascribed to foul weather and bureaucratic ineptitude. Those tragedies are always well attended by debris and rescue squads and grim-looking television news crews who are secretly elated by the *great fucking visuals* (a direct quote).

What happens goes something like this: You leave for work in the morning and on your return there is the peeling arbutus, with the tire swing still dangling from the lowest branch, the rope slightly frayed but not so much you've ever noticed. There's the cedar hedge that hid the partially disassembled Triumph Twin in the carport that you will now never ride down the I-5 to the Coast Highway, cruising all the way to Eureka to visit that chowder shack where you first met (so never mind that the clam chowder tasted like it had been stewed in an ashtray, you'll always remember it as ambrosia). There's the empty koi pond—so incompatible with the wandering black bears and the fat, happy raccoons—with ghost fish flickering in the shallows. The upturned blue box is still at the curb. And in the spot where the house once stood is a long, dull pucker, a barely perceptible seam where the earth has hastily knit itself together.

And no insurance policy in the world with a clause to cover what has happened.

Honey Fortunata (her real name) sings "Sweet Dreams (Are Made of This)" as she manoeuvres her new lease-to-own Hummer along Georgia towards the Lions Gate Bridge. It's been her anthem, practically a mantra, ever since she heard it on Martha Stewart's *Apprentice*. "Everybody's looking for thomething ..." The slightest trace of an accent—people often mistake it for a lisp—creeps into her voice whenever she's feeling emotional.

There are those who would view the Hummer as capitulation, but Honey tends to look on the bright side—that's how she stays afloat. She kept what her favourite British children's stories called *a stiff upper lip* when her mother left seven-year-old Honey with her grandmother in Davao City and flew fifteen time zones across the Pacific to take care of another woman's children. The lip barely quivered at age fourteen when she didn't even recognize her own mother on the international arrivals level of the Vancouver airport, or the six-year-old girl who, her mother told Honey, was her sister. That same lip, encased in sensible matte-finish Taupe by MAC, stayed the course when her mother died and when her little sister, Charity, decided that sliding her crotch up and down the pole at No. 5 Orange was preferable to attending classes at Van Tech Secondary while Honey worked days sorting processed meats into neat stacks at Subway and studying nights for her real estate licence.

Let the other agents travel in packs like cowardly hyenas or teenaged boys with pants riding the barrens of their non-existent buttocks. Let them retreat in fear, taking jobs in felt-lined cubicles on the nineteenth floor of a securities company. Honey Fortunata, snug in her Kevlar pantsuit, behind the wheel of her bulletproof high-mobility multi-purpose vehicle (civilian version), is on her way to close on the $7-million-plus split-level on Decourcy Court. And no thwarted buyer taking potshots at real estate agents is going to stop her. She even has the RE/MAX logo on the driver's side door—the #1 in *We're #1 in West Van!* forming what could be construed as a perfect bull's eye at her left breast.

From her dashboard, above the combat-grade instrument cluster with its eerily glowing global-positioning device, a hollow plastic Virgin Mary filled with holy water from Cap-de-la-Madeleine, hands open at her sides, smiles wryly at Honey as if to say, *Let me tell you about stiff upper lip.*

It's difficult to say just how badly Nina is sweating inside her Olympic mascot costume, as even under ideal circumstances she is the Lance Armstrong of perspiration. If there were an Olympic medal for sweating, there she'd be, on the tier of the podium closest to heaven, her Athens-vintage Roots singlet plastered to her body, brandishing gold. She blames her Eastern European heritage, something hirsute and unfavourable embedded in her twist of DNA, combined with a childhood of pork fat, too many root vegetables, and polyester stretch pants. Yet there is something distinctly working class about excess sweat, which is why she's never followed up on her mother's suggestion (may she squirm in eternal unrest) that she have some of her eccrine glands removed. I secrete therefore I am, Nina liked to scoff. And really, is there anything more bourgeois than elective surgery?

This is where a lifelong commitment to battling environmental degradation has led her. She is a thirty-eight-year-old woman lumbering around Granville Island Public Market dressed like a roly-poly Vancouver Island marmot, an animal that in real life is about to tip into the abyss, but who crookedly grins from all the banners spanning the city's bridges, and whose smaller but no less roly-poly Beanie Baby™ version is clutched by American and British and German and Japanese children passing through upgraded security at the Vancouver International Airport, children who (kids will be kids) Olympics organizers are counting on to relentlessly badger their parents to bring them back four years from now for the Games (cue visual of Eternal Flame).

Community service, they call it. Her week-long jail sentence has been commuted to this: a month of waddling through zombie-like crowds anaesthetized by all manner of smoked salmon tidbits. Nina waves in what she's decided is a jaunty

manner, while giving the finger from safely inside a fat, plush
paw to anyone who has a sharp crease ironed into her professionally laundered jeans or looks even remotely aware of what
a stock option is. Armies of pigeons swoop low overhead at
regular intervals in eerily coordinated phalanxes. Toddlers
lurch erratically at the birds that land on the wharf outside the
market. Gulls screech and dive for rogue french fries with the
precision of heat-seeking missiles. In the distance, a guitarist is
trying to bring a Roberta Flack tune back from the dead. There
are many who call this paradise.

Two teenaged girls stop in front of Nina. It's fall already,
but they wear halter tops, nipples on high alert like shark fins
patrolling the dangerous fabric, and too much kohl, making
their porcine eyes look even smaller and meaner. By now sweat
has puddled in Nina's sneakers, moisture squelching between
her toes as if she's been traipsing through Burns Bog. She still
has over an hour left to go. One of the girls starts poking at
Nina's marmot belly. "He's soooo cute! Aren't you cute?" The
girl makes her mouth go all round and tight and bends over,
feigning a blow job. The other one holds her sides and shrieks
in that way only fourteen-year-old girls can.

To hell with this. Nina wants to whack them, to wreak
revenge for tens of thousands of bus passengers and moviegoers
who've been held hostage over the years by potty-mouthed,
hysterically shrieking adolescent girls, and in fact raises a
padded hand to swat at them—already picturing the crowd
parting like the Red Sea while some heroic German tourist, a
Heinz, a muscled tool-and-die maker from Mönchweiler, drops
his smoked salmon kebab or salmon fajita and springs forward
to wrestle the crazed Olympic mascot to the ground (Sayonara,
community service! Hello, jail!)—when, at the outer edge of her
field of vision, which is pretty limited considering the marmot

head and the sweat stinging her eyes, she sees Dan and Patricia O'Donnell. Not a couple with a vague resemblance to the pair in the magazine ad, but them. Or a perfect simulacrum.

Patricia is sniffing a fennel bulb. She holds it out to Dan and then laughs as the licorice-scented fronds tickle his nose and he lightly shakes his head. The moment looks scripted (cue tinkling laughter), and Nina can't help but glance over her shoulder for a camera crew and klieg lights. A small boy in a private-school uniform stands between them, reaching for the fennel. As the three walk away, hand in hand, a luminous arc of white light envelops them. A trick of the late-afternoon sun.

No. A vision. But Nina, who's been a determined unbeliever for years, no longer has the vaguest notion of what it means to be confronted by a vision.

How can we measure disbelief? How many cubic tonnes of topsoil and almost impenetrable glacial till and granitic bedrock must be removed without recovering a single wall stud, newel post, or fragment of ceramic tile, how far into the substrata must workers delve without a trace of the chef-quality Amana gas range or the collection of stubby beer bottles (bought at auction), how many heavy-equipment operators must make limp jokes about digging a hole all the way to China and shake their heads at the homeowners' evident derangement as they ask them to excavate just one metre deeper, how many times must their daughter sob, But I don't want a new Costa-Rica-Survivor Barbie™, I want *my* Costa-Rica-Survivor Barbie™, before the bereft owners—who cringe at anything that smacks of the supernatural, pretend to gag at the words *chakra* and *aura*, and roll eyes skyward when anyone speaks of faith— must accept the unfathomable? Their house, all 3,217 square feet of it, and its entire contents have vanished without a trace.

Then there's the dog. A formerly amiable wheaten terrier who circles the perimeter of the yawning pit, endlessly snuffling at the loose earth, snapping at anyone who comes near, possibly mourning in his canine brain a soggy tennis ball left on the mat by the back door, or a beloved chew toy (the peppermint-scented Orbee bone) that felt so good against his aging gums, or simply an ambient memory of a sweet spot in the master bedroom where the late-afternoon September sun edged through the skylight and onto the kilim rug where he wasn't technically allowed but where he whiled away the empty hours in a kind of existential bliss.

Dan and Patricia are everywhere, spreading like toxic mould. On the No. 14 bus on Hastings a few days ago, Patricia looked primly at Nina from the dimly backlit panel ad, eyebrows winched skyward, as Nina glared back. If you're looking for the best of everything, sister, you're on the wrong bus. Dan still had his smirk, but didn't meet her eyes. He looked out past her at a young woman wearing a *Happy Planet* T-shirt that appeared to have been designed for an eight-year-old and shakily crunching Doritos, sallow pad of her stomach overexposed between the well-worn shirt and her low-riders, studded white belt pockmarked with cigarette burns, a rail yard criss-crossing her inner arms. Nina could've sworn Dan had to adjust his pants at the crotch.

Even the billboard at the entrance to Granville Island, just the other day advertising the delights of the Vancouver Aquarium and its imprisoned beluga population, now shows the couple, toothy smiles set on stun, in their kitchen, an assault of stainless-steel surfaces and grey-blue slate. Patricia is poised to slice a fennel bulb. The knife in her hand glints under halogen light while Dan leans across the cooking island as if whispering something naughty in her ear. Here's the really weird thing. They look less like Dan and Patricia than the real Dan and Patricia Nina saw last week on the wharf outside the market.

It's only much later, when she's trying to get back to sleep around four A.M.—the time she often wakes and can't remember which side of her chest houses her heart, even though it's thrumming so violently she fears the landlady will start pounding on the floor above her bed, yelling, "I thought I told you to keep it down!"—that it dawns on Nina: the real Dan and Patricia O'Donnell were not Caucasian like the actors in the ad, but Chinese. Tall for Chinese, but unmistakably Chinese. Odd that she hadn't noticed at the time.

Never make the mistake of showing how much you really want something. That's Honey's philosophy. She reels in uncommitted buyers by appealing to their unclothed desires. If you want four competing bids above list price on your aging ranch-style on Eagle Harbour Road, go ahead and give Honey Fortunata a call. Because Honey knows what to watch for and Honey doesn't talk too much.

That childless couple in their mid-thirties, the wife who hovers a little too long in the doorway of a second bedroom? That fifty-eight-year-old civil engineer who seems disproportionately interested in the empty carriage house out back and mentions having gone to the Emily Carr Institute of Art and Design a lifetime ago? Honey knows just what to do. She calls them to come and take a second look; the sellers are very motivated (real estate code for getting a divorce).

The couple returns, and when the wife looks into the bedroom again she sees a pine crib with an Anne Geddes photograph above it of a baby dressed like a bumblebee. The room smells of talcum powder and a limitless future. Bewildered, she turns to Honey and says, "I didn't notice a baby's room before!" Honey smiles. "You went through so quickly last time." The workaholic engineer returns to find the carriage house partially transformed into a painting studio, stretched canvases and splotches everywhere. "Excuse the mess," Honey says, shrugging, "but the owner has this little hobby."

But even Honey makes mistakes. That day two months ago when she finally tracked down Charity—her sister walking along Blood Alley with the herky-jerky marionette steps of an addict, small, untethered breasts straining against her *Happy Planet* T-shirt, while Honey negotiated with her pimp and dealer. He told her Charity had ripped off some very scary people and was alive only because of his personal munificence (although he called it something less poetic), and Honey had said, "Name your price."

Nina holds a pair of ski poles awkwardly in her lumpy paws and pretends to slalom in slow motion through the Granville Island crowd watching Byron-from-England, a flame-haired, flame-juggling comedian who specializes in homophobic jibes. People step back to clear Nina a path and smile good-naturedly; children point and yell: "A bear!" (The marmot is actually a rodent, but no one on the Olympic Committee wanted kids pointing and yelling, "A rat!" so they've erred on the side of the ursine. After all, who, except for those trying to save the doomed Vancouver Island marmot, has actually ever seen one?) But there's this one guy, a large man eating fries from a paper cone, who doesn't budge. Just gives her a look Nina knows all too well because she's seen it staring back at her in pale, aggrieved reflection from SkyTrain and shop windows and her own bathroom mirror.

The noise in her head is like one of those fireworks kids

launch all through the night at Halloween, a high-pitched squealer that ends, not quite with a bang, but with a loud pop. *Greetings, fellow misanthrope, now get the hell out of my way!*

She heads straight for the French Fry Guy as if he's the finish line, ski poles flailing to the left, to the right, to the left. A woman yells, "Curtis!" and yanks a Jack Russell on an extendable leash out of Nina's way. Poles high in the air now, well over her head, sweat coursing from her armpits like ill-fated bison streaming over the last rise at Head-Smashed-In Buffalo Jump. With a warrior cry, Nina slams into the man and bounces backwards off him as if she's a character in a Saturday-morning cartoon. You can practically hear the requisite *Boing!*

"Mascot busts a move!" someone announces, DJ-style. Nina's head should be cracked open, her durian fruit of a brain fouling the sea-spiked air, but the marmot suit has cushioned the fall. She staggers to her feet to scattered applause, woo-hoos!, and the insistent, machine-gun laughter of someone going off his meds. The salmon eaters think it was all part of her act.

As she straightens, Nina sees the same little boy in the private-school uniform from last week standing in front of her, like a miniature security guard in his blazer with its cheesy golden crest. The light behind his head is dazzling, reminding her that it hasn't rained for several weeks; the reservoirs are unusually low, and residents have been asked to share baths and take short showers. Dan and Patricia no doubt still fill their Jacuzzi tub to the brim, hot water tumbling unchecked from the gilded modernist faucet. Nina pictures Dan sliding in behind Patricia, kneading the knots in the small of her back as she releases a tight little sigh, reluctantly, as if she'd never willingly let go of anything.

The sun fires the tips of the boy's hair into a spiky penumbra, a hazy crown of thorns. He gazes up at Nina with something approximating concern in his eyes and reaches out.

A little hand in hers. It would be so easy.

Of course, there are those who say, "The mountain is angry." The disappearances of the North Shore houses now number in the high hundreds, and as downtown hotels fill up with the moneyed homeless, letters to the local papers speak of Gaia's revenge or God's displeasure. To voice these kinds of beliefs in the wake of the Asian tsunami or Hurricane Katrina would have invited instant censure. But here the victims are people of means, not the already downtrodden, so the notion that they're being either cosmically punished or held up as "a warning to us all?" (*Vancouver Sun* editorial, October 16, 2006) is debated in the mainstream media by pundits with straight faces.

And that slurry of twittering that can be heard around every corner? That'd be the sound of *schadenfreude*.

Unlike those who act as if they're on speed-dial to the Earth goddess—those men on recumbent bikes and those women who rub baking soda into their fuzzy armpits and think fetal-monitoring machines are the work of the devil—rational-ists who've always harboured a secret penchant for Greek mythology know full well that Gaia is in fact the daughter of Chaos.

Still, there is talk of healing. The chief of the Squamish Nation is invited to say a few words over the deep hole where a house had stood, a place that was once tribal land. The event evolves into something rather ecumenical, with smudge sticks, button blankets, trickster stories, and didgeridoos. As a dog howls forlornly, the elder quotes from Chief Seattle's famous 1854 speech. "It is the order of nature, and regret is useless. Your time of decay may be distant, but it will come, for even the White Man ... We may be brothers after all. We will see."

And the mountain in answer? Not so much as a burp.

"I didn't know marmots could drive!" The boy twists and turns in the passenger seat of Nina's car, punctuating each breathless pronouncement with body language. He has proved to have an insatiable appetite for all things marmot and an endless arsenal of exclamation marks. It's as if he's cornered the market on enthusiasm and is doling it out without regard for the niceties of supply and demand.

Nina envisions the look on Patricia's face as she turns from applauding Byron-from-England's Houdini-like escape from a straitjacket and padlocked chain to find her Cracker Jack prize of a son gone, and feels a rare frisson of self-satisfaction.

She is finding it hard to keep her paws on the steering wheel, and shoulder-checking is impossible with the mascot head still on. She doesn't usually drive if she can help it and her mid-'70s Toyota Corolla is practically in its death throes, but this morning she was running late after a savage bout of insomnia, and trying to make her shift by bus was not an option. The walk back to her car, parked on a side street just outside Granville Island, felt impossibly long, with the boy chittering away at her side as he trotted to match her pace. But there were remarkably few people about and she's fairly certain no one saw them get in the car and pull away.

It seems he's only in kindergarten—what kind of people would put a five-year-old in a uniform, complete with blazer?— and that his teacher, whose name sounds something like Miss Peach (the boy talks so fast Nina can't make out everything he's saying), has made the Vancouver Island marmot the official class animal. "There's only about a hundred of you left in existence!"

Nina nods. She tells him she's come to the city as an ambassador for her fellow marmots, to make people understand that they have to stop hacking away at the old-growth forests and destroying their habitat.

"And they sent you because you're the biggest!!"

"And because I'm the only one who could drive a standard," Nina says as the car shudders onto her street just off Commercial Drive. Breathing in her own expelled carbon dioxide in the confines of the car is making her giddy, as if her brain cells are multiplying too rapidly, spawning an overpopulated subsidized-housing project in her skull cavity.

In front of the just-completed reno on the corner, a hired gun in a surgical mask is blowing leaves from the lawn and the sidewalk with a backpack blower. They gust madly, whirling like the calendar pages in *Citizen Kane* before settling into the gutter. Nina can remember when there was a clear divide in the city, a line in the sand all parties respected. West of Main was where you found the leaf blowers, east of Main people still retained a genetic memory of how to wield a rake and a broom. But when property prices started spiking wildly there began a drift of Westside sensibilities into her formerly bohemian and Italian neighbourhood, along with their implements of destruction.

"Satan's little helper," she says.

"What?" says the boy.

"The two-stroke terrorist." She points towards the leaf blower.

The boy's eyes go wide. "My dad has one of those."

She doesn't answer, letting him draw his own conclusions. The boy sucks in his lips until his mouth disappears. Nina can feel the sweat pooling in her ears as the car grinds to a stop in front of her place.

It's the leaf blowers that undo her every time. They're the reason she's trapped in this sauna-hell of a mascot costume in the first place. That day in late August, as Nina hurried along Napier to her shift at the food co-op, there was a woman out in front of the new heritage-style infill that towered over its neighbours; she was blasting a blower back and forth across her lawn as if she were divining for water. With her tidy silver-grey pageboy and batiked sarong wrapped around her sturdy, late-middle-aged body, she exuded an obnoxious serenity. The grass, smooth as a green sheet yanked tight over the yard and tucked in with hospital corners, appeared spotless save for a few stray leaves from a Japanese maple. Nina stopped, ignoring the warning in her head that was whooping like a car alarm, and stood on the sidewalk with her hands on her hips.

"I thought you might like to know," she said loudly over the ear-splitting roar of the blower, "a leaf blower causes as much air pollution as seventeen cars!" The woman didn't even glance her way. Nina strode onto the lawn, yelling, "I said, *I thought you might like to know that a leaf blower causes as much air pollution as seventeen cars!*"

The woman trained the nozzle on the one remaining red leaf, which quivered slightly but stayed where it was. Nina wrenched the leaf blower out of the woman's hands and aimed it at her face. The pageboy lifted off the startled woman's scalp before she could grab it. The wig hovered overhead for a few seconds like an antediluvian bird before blowing off and snagging on a bare branch of the maple. The woman stood there, impossibly wide-eyed and bald, an anime character, as Nina screamed about carcinogens and decibel levels and the end of civilization while wielding the leaf blower like an AK-47. Later, Nina would recall that this was the moment she understood how something like Columbine could happen.

The woman pulled pale pink wax plugs from her ears and, backing away slowly, said, "I'm going to call 911." Or maybe just mouthed the words before Nina lunged.

Honey sings to maintain her equilibrium, "Thome of them want to use you, thome of them want to get used by you ...," her long, black hair blowing across her face in the breeze from across the water. Driving over the Lions Gate Bridge always tightens her guts, but not as badly as crossing the Second Narrows does. That one, she's determined, is just plain bad luck. The Ironworkers Memorial Second Narrows Crossing, as it's officially designated, a name no one uses, was consecrated in blood. Whenever Honey traverses it she makes the sign of the cross in deference to the dead. The last time she took that route to the North Shore, she lifted her hands off the steering wheel at the halfway point and veered into the next lane, almost clipping a motorcyclist with a helmetless passenger.

Her older friend Judit's father was one of the workers who died when the bridge collapsed during construction, Judit fresh in the womb, her mother maddened by the loss. Judit dreams every so often of falling men, she's told Honey, *men falling from the sky like bad rain, like laundry.*

Dear Judit, who still works at the Subway franchise where they met, despite her advanced cake-decorating certificate from the Pacific Institute of Culinary Arts and her uncanny ability to retain statistical information. She doesn't have Honey's drive (as Judit's admitted more than once, with admiration but not envy), which is of the old-fashioned sort, almost Presbyterian in its austerity. Honey has never taken a vacation, doesn't have time to devote to dating, and still lives in the salmon-coloured stucco townhouse under the SkyTrain line near Nanaimo Station she'd shared with her late mother and Charity, the trains juddering overhead at intervals as reassuringly regular as her paycheques. But Honey is nothing if not aspirational. And when she launches her home-decor shop after this Decourcy Court sale closes, she'll have jobs for Judit and her sister. Jobs that allow you to lift your chin sky high, *you can bet your sweet bippy*, as Judit liked to say.

Far above Honey, the lights strung along the Lions Gate's suspension cables, *Gracie's pearls*, haven't winked on yet. When night comes they'll resume their siren call to distressed souls.

Just last week, another suicidal person jumped from the bridge to the absolution of the frigid waters below. Honey believes in fortitude, but fortitude is sometimes not enough. This is why the Blessed Virgin filled with holy water stands on her state-of-the-art dash. Honey likes to cover all her bases. You can bet your sweet bippy.

"Is this where you live?" the boy asks as they round the side of the house to the entrance that leads to Nina's basement suite. She tries to see it through his over-privileged little eyes. The back fence, chicken wire, sags low with the weight of accumulated morning glory, now dying, revealing a rutted back alley strewn with KFC carcasses the raccoons have freed from garbage bags. There's more than one abandoned upholstered chair, the stuffing festively mounding out like popcorn.

Next door, her neighbour, a well-muscled, mulleted thirty-something on permanent disability from complications involving a cuckolded husband and an illegal firearm, practises his nanchukas. He's part of a subterranean tribe of basement dwellers that emerge blinking into the mid-afternoon light from their illegal suites like small nocturnal animals long after those with more conventional circadian rhythms have scattered for the day.

"Cool," the boy says.

The man looks over and grins, wiggling his Fu Manchu moustache. "Wherever you go, there you are." The guy has a paperback of Carlos Castaneda's *The Teachings of Don Juan* spread-eagled on a vinyl lawn chair beside an ashtray, a roach clip holding the still-smouldering twist of a joint perched on its rim. He tokes for medicinal purposes, he's confided to Nina more than once, as if she gives a shit. As if every second house on the street wasn't a grow-op. Nina is tempted to tell him she's the one who blew the whistle on the operation the Grow Busters pot squad raided two blocks over last year, the one that turned out to be a federally licensed medical-marijuana site—even though this isn't true. She just wants to knock the co-conspirator look off his face, the one he always gives her when they happen to come up out of their suites at the same time.

He either doesn't notice or doesn't care that Nina is dressed like an oversized rodent, but he's very interested in the sharp kirpan fastened to the boy's belt. There's also a cloth covering the small bun on the boy's head. A *patka*, a sort of pre-turban turban for Sikh youths, the boy explained to Nina in the car, as she madly tried to recollect if his parents had looked even remotely South Asian. When had she stopped looking at people, really looking rather than simply noticing the things about them that drove her crazy?

"Little man, they let you wear that to school?" the neighbour asks. The boy pulls free the dagger and starts citing some B.C. Supreme Court case. "So, when you have a culturally diverse society," he concludes, "rights and obligations sometimes conflict!"

He doesn't realize she's not a real marmot, but he can sum up a legal argument as if reciting a nursery rhyme. Nina wonders, not for the first time, whether the child is some kind of idiot savant.

The guy shows the boy how to wield the nanchukas, holding one wooden stick firmly in his fist while deftly manipulating the one on the other end of the connecting chain. The boy makes a feeble pass at twirling the weapon, while the guy carves the air with the kirpan.

"Careful," he says. "I've kunked myself more than once and my head's probably a lot thicker than yours."

Dwayne, Darrin, Dork? Nina has lived beside him for eight years and still can never remember his name.

It should be mentioned that the mountain has not swallowed a single sentient being. The disappearances never occur when anyone is at home. The mountain has an uncanny sense of timing. The nanny will have just rounded the corner with the twins when she remembers she should have packed the rain cover for the stroller. She turns back. I was only gone for a minute, she'll say later, looking heavenward, crossing herself over and over as if she has a nervous tic.

Cockatiels, cats, dogs, hamsters, boa constrictors, and, once, a miniature goat—all manner of bewildered pets have been recovered at the scenes of the disappearances. The only human witness, a girl of four who had been left to play in the sandbox while her older sister took care of business with the boy next door, has been rendered mute. When asked to explain what happened, she forms a cup with her hands and smiles beatifically. The experts say post-traumatic stress disorder, while her mother insists her ADHD has been cured.

Does anyone remember that aggrieved musician of Hamelin Town? Can anyone besides this enraptured girl hear his cunning tune?

Honey Fortunata is turning onto the Caulfeild exit off the Upper Levels when her cellphone rings—no "La Macarena," no Beethoven's Fifth, for Honey is not a person who indulges in whimsy. As she listens to the voice at the other end, Honey's lip begins to tremble so hard she has to press two fingers to her mouth to still it. The house on Decourcy, the one she was just about to close on, has joined the ranks of the disappeared.

Honey snaps shut her cell and pulls over. She takes increasingly shallow breaths and watches as her commission on $7.4 million does this funny thing. It sprouts wings, white, downy ones like a Catholic schoolgirl's version of an angel, and flits up and out of the Hummer, right through the windshield as if the glass were permeable, then hovers for a moment above the gleaming hood before tumbling up into the unnaturally clear sky, along with Honey's chances of buying back her sister's life.

A clear, operatic soprano sings out, startling the silence. Honey fumbles with the stereo, but the music is not coming from the speakers. For the first time in her life a thing very much like the chokehold of fear closes around her throat. The aria is coming from the Virgin Mary on the dashboard—her voice like a young Jessye Norman singing "Ave Maria." What look to be real tears trickle from the icon's painted blue eyes and Honey finds that she, too, is crying.

Nina wakes from what must have been a catnap; there's still some light coming through the ground-level windows. Her head is muzzy, the inside of the mascot suit a moist cave, no doubt incubating new single-cell life forms by now. The TV is on, *The Simpsons* in perpetual rerun just ending—Lisa has saved Springfield again and wears yet another medal bestowed by the mayor. As the boy sits static in front of the set, the evening news leads with a missing-child story.

Dan's face is slack, a spent stocking. Please don't hurt our son. But Patricia. She looks straight at Nina and threatens to rip her entrails out. Not so much in words but in an understanding that passes between them like a kind of heat. Patricia's teeth now a serval cat's, a guttural hiss issuing from deep in her throat. Nina's striated flesh already clings to Patricia's yellowed incisors and she's crunching down on her bones as if they're pretzels. Muscles roll like small ball bearings under the skin of her jaws.

"I never knew my dad was such a good actor!" the boy says with evident admiration. "But Mom … " He sighs and shrugs his shoulders, palms turned up, like a badly mugging child star, Jonathan Lipnicki maybe, without the owlish glasses. Nina has told him his parents had been enlisted by Miss Peach to go along with the pretend kidnapping in order to bring media attention to the marmot cause.

"You have a very nice burrow here, you know!" he tells her as he waits patiently in front of the TV for any word about the official class animal.

Nina rummages through the cupboards, looking for something a child might want to eat. Clumsy paws knock a large jar of pickled beets to the floor. Glass pierces beet flesh, vivid purplish-red juice spills everywhere. "Fuck!"

The boy looks up from his vigil on the floor. "You're not really a marmot, are you?"

She tries to whistle through her teeth. He's informed her— more than once already—that the Vancouver Island marmot has a singular whistle when it's in distress.

Nina sits down on the floor across from the boy and twists off the mascot head, the frigid basement air hitting her face and neck, skin instantly congealing, skin shrink-wrapping her bones as it dries. "You're not really a child, are you?"

On the news there's a story about another one of those disappeared houses and an aerial shot of the North Shore starting to look as unpopulated as it did back in the 1950s, or so the reporter says, in a way that implies this is somehow a bad thing.

The boy lifts the marmot head from Nina's lap and plops it onto his own head.

Years later, when Nina looks back on all of this, which will be less often than you might think, it's not the feral hatred in Patricia's eyes or Dan's crumpled sock-puppet face that she remembers, but this, a boy's small hands gripping the matted plush of the marmot head to keep it from toppling off, his breath amplified inside the cave of the mesh skull, and inside her own skull the echo of the insistent plink, plink, plink from the bathtub faucet that never stops dripping, the grunts of her neighbour through the thin walls as he hurtles exotic weapons at an unseen enemy, her mother's laughter, jostling Nina's head as it lay in her lap, when the nun held up the Nazis' distributor cap and said, "Reverend Mother, I have sinned," while the cathode glaze of the late-night movie washed over them, mother and daughter, the bowl holding the crumbled remains of ripple chips on the coffee table, and the Family von Trapp escaping, yet again, over the Alps to Switzerland, to asylum, to a type of freedom in neutrality, and Nina, then only seven, maybe eight, not really thinking, not knowing, that maybe life would never get better than this.

The boy exudes such calm despite his proclivity to exclamation. Maybe all children are like this in private. She could surround herself with more children. She could be like that old woman who keeps hundreds of cats who will feast on her body when she dies, scrapping over the choice bits, the desiccated liver, tender, swollen kidneys ballooning up around her spine, her heart like a dime, cold and thin.

Then, a muffled "Pee-yoo! It really stinks in here!"

On the news, an impeccably dressed woman with long, dark hair curtaining her face falls to her hands and knees, scrabbling at the earth with her bare hands, flinging hunks of sod through the air and keening while onlookers watch from a safe distance beyond the gaping hole in the ground. A huge vehicle, like the ones U.S. soldiers used during Desert Storm, is parked behind her, engine still thrumming, door ajar, a red, white, and blue RE/MAX sign on its side. Somewhere, someone is cocking a rifle. Somewhere, someone is singing a haunting aria.

It's about the things you want. Don't let anyone tell you differently. It's about the things you can't have.

Is it so terrible to want what you can't have? Can someone tell Nina that? Huh, huh,

huh, huh? Anyone?

THE ADOPTED CHINESE DAUGHTERS' REBELLION

This much we know. Across the playing fields just east of the Jericho Beach Youth Hostel they hobbled, some of them holding hands, Mei Li and Xiao Yu for sure, yes, they would have been holding hands—fingers threaded together in a tight weave, like a waterproof basket made of reeds bobbing along an irrigation canal, a baby girl wrapped in newspaper mewling inside. The other girls hurried alongside them. Mei Ming would have started singing; she was the musical one, the one with *that voice*, as we often heard the mothers of the other girls grudgingly admit.

They stopped halfway across the field. We can tell you that. The moon that night was a fat crescent, like a window on an outhouse door in a *New Yorker* cartoon. Their strange footprints must have shimmered in the fresh snow. *A herd of deer*, an early-morning dog walker might have thought, *how odd*.

How much odder the truth.

A number of the girls appear to have eaten chocolate bars, miniature Caramilks no doubt left over from Halloween, the wrappers casually tossed near the second baseline of the ball diamond. One of them smoked a cigarette, a Matinée Extra Mild, the butt found lightly rimmed in marzipan-scented Lip Smacker where the footprints abruptly ended. Another wrote *Up yours* in the snow, not with swaggering piss the way a boy would have, but by clumsily dragging her small heel. (*Not my daughter*, Frank de Rocherer insisted the next morning, stamping his slipper-clad foot—in their panic most of the parents hadn't thought to get dressed. As if that mattered now, which daughter smoked, which daughter was profane, which daughters had insatiable sweet tooths.)

From a distance, if you approached the snowy field from the west, their footprints looked like a series of brushstrokes forming a long-necked bird. *A crane*, Myra Nagle insisted, and soon that's what it was, a crane rising skyward. A most auspicious symbol, we have since learned.

Of course we weren't there to witness all this. We can only imagine. Conjecture, you understand. And if it hadn't been for the snowfall, a rare Christmas Eve snowfall in the coastal city, we wouldn't have anything to go on at all.

THE YEAR OF THE STORK

We watched, those of us who were too old, too divorced, too medicated (too selfish, some said, too *lazy*) to have adopted Chinese daughters. We watched some dozen years ago as couples living on our cul-de-sac disappeared into the smog-cloaked air of Guangdong Province—one of the most polluted places on earth, where the clang and clatter of an almost desperate progress hearkened back to Dickensian England—and returned with tiny, clear-eyed girls whose provenance was a mystery, known only to the hollow-armed mothers who had forsaken them, and whose only forms of identification, besides the *Resident alien* stamps beside their names in their new passports, were the ragged pieces of rice paper, marked with their footprints in red ink, that their new parents framed behind glass and hung above their cribs in white bedrooms overlooking the ocean, as if to say, *Watch your step.*

We're making it sound as if all this happened seamlessly. In fact, ethical debates stormed through our cul-de-sac for an entire summer on the issue of bringing children into a world beset by woe, when more than a continent away dark-haired babies lay on greying sheets, their futures rapidly fraying at the edges.

We know most of the men cheerfully submitted to vasectomies. "Too much information," we'd say if we met them while hauling our blue boxes to the curb and they jocularly pointed out—although not before noting (once again) that we hadn't flattened our cans—that they'd spent the previous evening parked in front of the Discovery Channel sitting on a bag of frozen peas, adding that it was the least they could do to help save wear and tear on the planet. Or, as prematurely grey, ponytailed Gary Forsythe put it, making a peace sign and then scissoring his fingers much too close to our faces, *Snip snip.* The women were also aggressive about birth control, although even Carol Fawcett's closest friends admitted they found her opting for a full hysterectomy a little, well, "show-offy, don't you think?"

Jiang Li was first. "You should call her Pearl!" one of us exclaimed as we all crowded around for another look at those fingers, those toes. "Oh, no," said Laura Warkentin, scrunching up her face as if we'd suggested calling her daughter Rover or Spike. Her husband, Joe, standing behind her, recited a Chinese proverb: "Human beings are like falling water. Tip them East and they flow East. Tip them West and they flow West." He sounded like Master Po addressing the young Kwai Chang Caine in *Kung Fu*. At the time we thought he was just trying to be amusing.

We found it touching at first how Jiang Li's parents offered a wealth of detail about the circumstances of her abandonment. Wrapped in elephant-leaved taro and left by an irrigation canal in the Pearl River Delta, water buffalo in a neighbouring field looking as if they were standing guard, an illegible note pinned to her diaper. But as our formerly quiet street swelled with the sounds of cooing and crying, the oft-repeated stories became overwhelming, like some life-sized game of Clue run amok. Xin Qian by a freeway bundled in a pair of worn blue work pants. Fang Yin on a bench in a moonlit park clutching the stub of a movie ticket (*Flashdance*). Li Wei at a railroad station teething on a wizened yam.

It was as if where they were found explained who they were. As if looking back was more important than looking forward. As if there was something intrinsically romantic, rather than profoundly disturbing, about a baby found at an open-air market in a cardboard box amidst a pile of pole beans or winter melons.

THE FENG SHUI OF ANDREW MACINTOSH

We watched, those of us who lacked the emotional fortitude, the capacity for sacrifice, and the largeness of spirit (the *chutzpah*, some said, meaning it, of course, in the ecumenical sense) of our neighbours who had adopted Chinese daughters.

We watched Nina Sawatsky mastering homemade pot-stickers, brushing away our compliments with a breezy, "Oh, you know, they're just like perogies." We watched Jamie Tate patiently guiding his girl through her calligraphy exercises, until her brushstrokes were swift and sure, promising her a Shar-Pei puppy if she could master the character for bliss. We watched as Caitlin Rogers (yes, *those* Rogerses), holding her straight, honey-blond hair out of the way, showed her small daughter how to clear her throat and release a frothy gob curbside, just as the girl's ancestors had done for thousands of years (according to primary sources Caitlin Rogers herself had interviewed at the Chinese Benevolent Association on Pender Street). We watched Andy MacIntosh, a ruddy Scot, standing amidst the rubble of his house, his family ensconced at the Westin Bayshore, while he directed a construction team to favourably reorient their mock Tudor so the wind could blow through it in a manner that maximized the flow of positive ch'i, and to set the doors at an angle to the sidewalk so as to thwart evil spirits. (We were surprised to learn evil spirits were so easy to fool.) And he was just the first.

Feng shui, feng shui, feng shui—the cry rose and spread through our cul-de-sac like the swishing wings of a thousand cranes taking flight. The girls must have heard it, too. They held their hands to their ears; they each pulled a Sony Discman out of hiding places deep in the laurel bushes at the edge of the Gill-Campbell property, plugging themselves in as if to drown out the ancestral murmurs emanating from their newly situated houses.

We watched one particularly wet autumn morning just over a year ago as the girls, dressed in identical puffy quilted cotton jackets and worker pants, participated in group exercises out in the middle of the street, led by Marshall Evans. Their hair appeared to have been cut with pruning shears and was of a uniform, unflattering length. They were assigned households at random and sent off to greet their new parents and tidy their new bedrooms. The traditional-medicine phase of the summer—when the girls, bristling like porcupines, lay in their backyards on bamboo mats while Greig Ladner, a do-it-yourself kind of guy, applied his newly acquired acupuncture skills to everything from sunburns to hurt feelings—seemed so harmless now.

"Let a thousand flowers bloom," we suggested tactfully as we watched the girls form a human pyramid in order to clean out the eavestroughs on the Simpsons' stylish West Coast Modern, all the while singing patriotic marching songs praising Mao Tse-tung. "Oh, mind your own beeswax," said Dana Simpson, who was, we can be sure, echoing the sentiments of all the other parents.

We often wondered over the years what the girls really heard as they lay quietly in their beds at night in their embroidered silk pyjamas. There must have been something beyond the sharp clack of mah-jong tiles as their parents gathered around dining-room tables into the early hours of the morning, something just beyond the wind shivering through the thick stands of bamboo that obscured the view of the ocean from their bedroom windows. Something that made them continue to return their parents' hugs with a genuine fervour not born of that ancient curse called filial piety.

After everything that's happened, it must be said that we never heard the parents of the adopted Chinese daughters speak of undying gratitude; not once did they imply the girls owed them anything. It wasn't a matter of not enough love, but perhaps of too much. Any parent would understand.

That bamboo our neighbours planted turned out to be

highly resilient and invasive. We've been finding it everywhere lately—growing in the middle of a cedar deck, through a crack in the foundation of a garage. We need only lift the lid of a compost bin and a couple of rogue stalks spring forth, like something out of a 1950s horror movie. We've taken axes to the roots, flailing away until blisters rise on our palms. The roots themselves look prehistoric, like the skeletal remains of dinosaurs, curved vertebrae prickling, dry knobs of joints, and we feel strangely ashamed as we strain to pull them from the ground.

THE TAO OF LITTLE SUSANNA A.K.A. OOPS!

We watched, those of us with, admittedly, nothing better to do, as four years after the adopted Chinese daughters arrived on our cul-de-sac Bettina Lauridsen's belly began to grow. We watched as if witnessing something terribly transgressive, almost pornographic, although a casual observer at Choices Market on a Saturday morning would simply have noted a tired, pregnant brunette in her late thirties leaning on a cart while an alarmingly red-headed forty-something male scanned labels for MSG and a small Asian-featured girl tugged on her mother's jacket clamouring for a sugar-frosted cereal that was rumoured to be "Magically delicious!"

We threw a baby shower against Bettina L.'s protestations and invited all the mothers and their daughters. The girls were enchanted, especially Huan Yue, the sister-to-be. They pressed their palms to the tight bulge, their faces full of gravity and wonder, as if they were good fairies laying on a series of blessings, levitating the baby in its puddle of embryonic soup, while in the kitchen Darcas Conrad inverted an ice-cube tray over a bowl of guava punch and said, "Tubal ligation, my ass."

Her name was Susanna, or Oops!, as her parents took to calling her, except within earshot of her grandparents. We had legitimate concerns that little Susanna might be abandoned somewhere in accordance with our cul-de-sac's unofficial but implicit one-family-one-child policy. We watched for a woman sneaking out of the house under the cover of night and returning empty-handed, moth holes riddling her heart. But as time passed, it began to seem the little flame-haired girl was with us to stay.

The endearing thing about Susanna was that she wanted to be a Chinese daughter more than anything else. "Will I look like you when I grow up?" we heard her ask Huan Yue more than once, drooping when told she'd look exactly like herself.

She went door to door with a petition demanding her parents give her a Chinese name (meanwhile, we'd overheard the other girls secretly calling each other things like Krista, Madison, and Delaney). She begged to use chopsticks instead of a fork, to be allowed to practise Shaolin boxing with her sister, to learn Cantonese or even a little Mandarin. She drew little yin and yang symbols on her bare knees with indelible ink and was sent to her room to play with Florida Vacation Barbie™. And in the evenings, while her father diligently quizzed Huan Yue at the kitchen table about Chinese history ("The legendary woman warrior Mu Lan, unlike the Disney heroine, did not require the aid of a boyfriend," Peter O'Reilly often told us, as if we were the ones in need of a lesson), Susanna was banished to the den with a *Betty and Veronica Double Digest* and a mug of Ovaltine.

The day her parents caught little Susanna in the bathroom Scotch-taping up the corners of her eyes, they enrolled her in Irish step-dancing.

We've often wondered, is it a crime to want something you can't have? "She's a very clever girl," we assured each other.

"After all, she was born in the Year of the Monkey." Her father, overhearing, actually harrumphed, something most of us had only witnessed in cartoons. "She's a Taurus," he said, as if that was that.

THE I CHING OF KRIS KRINGLE

We watched, those of us who could no longer claim to understand the true meaning of Christmas, who had long stopped believing no two snowflakes are alike. We watched helplessly late last year as the adopted Chinese daughters, in their thirteenth year, at the foggy outskirts of their girlhood, set out to defy their parents.

In mid-November, Jiang Li and Fang Yin were found spray-painting frozen New Brunswick fiddleheads with gold Krylon while watching a Martha Stewart holiday special. Their daring served to embolden the others. Li Wei and Xin Qian skipped out on a horticultural tour at Dr. Sun Yat-Sen Garden to attend a performance of Handel's *Messiah* at Christ Church Cathedral (by all accounts, it was a very good year for the *Messiah*). Mei Li and Xiao Yu were caught exchanging gifts wrapped in paper embossed with trumpeting angels. Mei Ming was heard humming "Blue Christmas" in the tub, complete with the little Elvis hiccup. And Jiao Ping was spotted in front of Capers on 4th Avenue slipping the rumpled Salvation Army Santa a loonie.

A few days after it was discovered that Huan Yue had auditioned to play the Ghost of Christmas Yet to Come in the school pageant, we received (*FYI*, the attached Post-it notes read) a professionally rendered pamphlet in our mailboxes extolling the virtues of the ancient art of foot binding. Much was made of the cunning little embroidered boots the girls would wear, even to bed. Some of it was a bit too technical for us, with computer-generated diagrams detailing the length of cotton (4.57 metres) that would tightly bind the feet, the degree the four smaller toes were to be bent towards the sole (180), thereby breaking them, and how similar the bound foot is to a lotus blossom (very).

Traditionally, the mothers did the binding, but it appeared the girls' fathers were more than up to the task. Or as Nigel Kempton yelled through the open window of his planet-friendly family compact as he raced off to Fabricland, "Hey, women hold up half the sky, right?"

We didn't see much of the girls for the rest of December. Every so often a wan face would appear at a window, or we'd notice one of the daughters hobble to the car, leaning hard on her mother or father, heading to the doctor for a flu shot or to join one of the other families at Floata for dim sum. Susanna came and went, aiming big, angry kicks at the sodden leaves still mounded in the gutters, while her sister sat inside, her own feet growing as small as her circumstances.

Then on Christmas Eve, close to midnight, when most of us were already in bed, our doorbells began to chime. There on our steps stood the adopted Chinese daughters, begging to come in, to peer into the stockings tacked to our mantels, to shake a gift or two and puzzle over the muffled rattling inside, to sniff the nutmeg-scented air, to gaze at their own elongated reflections in the shiny balls that hung on the trees they'd glimpsed through our front windows, to snuggle by our hearths and confide they'd always dreamt each other's dreams and that they dreamt of the things they had done, or still wanted to do: sleep on ice floes, kiss the Queen's papery cheek, walk barefoot across burning sand to lay a humble gift inside a stable. To make us pay heed, they peeled their sweaters over their heads, revealing a startling array of undergarments (a puckered training bra, a bronze satin bustier, a frayed, sleeveless T-shirt that read *Remember Leon Klinghoffer*), and showed us the white pinfeathers erupting from their armpits in tidy rows.

It had already begun to snow and we noticed how otherworldly the girls' footprints appeared along our front walks. (Some of us later swore we saw little Susanna tumbling end over end across a snowy lawn with stunning alacrity, an illuminated Catherine wheel, her bare heels and tail spitting sparks.) We only said what seemed the right thing to say at the time, before closing our doors. "It's late. Go home."

Now we watch, all of us who had a hand in the fate of the adopted Chinese daughters and Susanna. We watch the sky for a flock of long-necked cranes and a flying monkey. It's early spring, but the houses on our cul-de-sac are decked out in full holiday regalia. There's even a reindeer on the roof of Huan Yue and Susanna's old house, Rudolph no less, its red nose a beacon that can be seen for miles. The lights on our houses are of the insistent blinking variety. The bulbs don't wink on and off at random, but blink in unison day and night.

Come back, come back, they whimper. *S.O.S.*

The other night we watched as one of the fathers bent to tidy a life-sized crèche, scooping handfuls of wet debris and a crumpled beer can from the manger where baby Jesus should have been. We began to wonder whether it was too late to ask what God might have to do with all this, but instead willed ourselves to think about the girls' footprints in that snowy field, and we marvelled, once again, at the effort it must have taken to walk even as far as they had.

WHAT ARE WE DOING HERE?

What is she doing here watching this older man, practically an old man, briskly rubbing garlic against the insides of a wooden bowl in preparation for a Caesar salad when she could be at a real party like the party last night where that one guy said he was so angry (angry!) at her for having such a beautiful butt he couldn't help smacking it with the flat of his hand, and then he did—so hard it stung Didi through her terry-cloth shorts, the same shorts that had everyone joking they should be using her as a hand towel, and didn't she finally let that freckle-faced little lesbian food stylist do just that to prove she had a sense of humour? The whole thing had been a riot, in fact, even though the butt-smacking guy had turned out to be an alarm salesman for a security company who lived out in Ajax and thought Rufus Wainwright (who was at the party, someone said, although she didn't see him with her own eyes) was *a famous racehorse*, so she couldn't go home with him. Could she?

It had been a rooftop party where you climbed out the kitchen window and then up the fire escape, so if you had to go to the bathroom you couldn't just bumble yourself down the hall and bang amiably on the door to dislodge some bashful substance abuser, you really had to want to go, although if you were a guy, let's say a butt-smacking alarm salesman who didn't wear a belt with his jeans (Rufus came in a *sarong*, someone said, although no one she knew actually saw him), you could piss into the base of a potted palm tree the hosts had lugged up onto the roof, with no doubt great difficulty, and strung with tiny lights resembling olives with pimento centres. And even though up until then Didi had encouraged the guy—even dribbled some of her martini down the front of his shirt, his handprint still a low-voltage buzz on her backside—after the incident with the palm tree, combined with the living-in-Ajax thing, the belt-loop thing, and the Rufus thing, she couldn't very well be seen with him and so she stayed long after he left with some overly loud girl in a Lycra T-shirt with a picture of Buddha on it and found herself waking up at about five-thirty this morning with roof pitch spotting her cheek as the sun was just starting to simmer behind the Gooderham & Worts building in the distance.

Now tonight, on a gas barbecue out on the old guy's balcony, two steaks sizzle and two enormous baked potatoes sit in their foil skins. There's not a tapenade or a small wrapped thingy in sight. Who eats food like this?

Excuse her for thinking this was going to be a *party* party or at least a dinner party with a few other people. After an hour of highballs and stilted conversation (during which Didi didn't know what else to do with her hands so she kept drinking and twisting the edge of her blouse until it looked like the snout of a small, angry, genetically altered monkey, and tried not to stare at the photographs lining the walls—all of older women, some extreme close-ups that turned their faces into what she imagines the baked surface of a Nevada desert looks like, and a few nudes in which skin falls towards earth like putty, like the women are melting, decomposing, in front of her eyes) she realizes no one else is coming, so she starts to wonder, not for the first time, what it would be like to sleep with a man this old, a man who could be fifty, maybe even fifty-five, and thinks she could stand it, that it would at least be an experience she could later use as a conversation piece, *a war story*. But he hasn't come on to her, at least not in the usual ways, although maybe older people do it differently. Why else would he have asked her here after she interviewed him last week for that mini-profile in the style section of *NOW*?

His forte, as she referred to it in her piece, was photographing aging female intellectuals, which Didi, personally, thinks is kind of perverse, although in her article she called him a feminist and praised him for loving women for their minds, because that's what the press release said—although she didn't believe it for a minute, especially when he insisted on calling her by her full name and invited her over, saying *Wear whatever you like, Deirdre* with feigned disinterest after she asked. She's wearing something filmy, a pastel-blue blouse that floats above her midsection (exposing the only tattoo-free stretch of twenty-three-year-old backside in the civilized world—her fear-of-pain thing neutralizing the humiliation she's entitled to feel over not having a kanji symbol or Celtic knot peeking out above her thong; even her nose ring is a clip-on). And just so no one would think she takes clothing that seriously, she's wearing track pants with the blouse, a combination she had hoped would keep them guessing, keep them wondering *what that Deirdre was all about*. But there's no *them* here, only him.

So last night there she was having such a great time, what with the terry-cloth-shorts thing and the butt-smacking thing and Rufus W. in his sarong there with his new boyfriend (who she thinks she did catch a glimpse of from the back after someone pointed him out), and now here she is watching a guy in brown plastic sandals, with his seriously yellowed toenails poking out for all the world to see, tossing a salad and telling her about the time he was sent to photograph the Berlin Wall coming down and how he was shocked at feeling a little sadness and nostalgia for Checkpoint Charlie and the *damn wall itself* (emphasis his) and how these feelings were so disturbing amidst the general euphoria that he just stood there as if paralyzed for a minute or two while champagne rained down on his head as if he were being baptized even though he didn't deserve it. And because there's nothing remotely flirtatious about this story and because she doesn't understand why he's telling her all this, Didi wants to ask, "What are we doing here?" It's the not knowing that's killing her. If nothing is going to happen, she's going to walk out right now, because what's the point of eating all these carbs and then just going home to watch some *Rhoda* reruns on WTN? That's what she'll be forced to do, as she can't very well go catch up with everyone—*the gang*—later and admit that the party she went to at the semi-famous photographer's place was a bust.

The interview last week had been fun. The photographer had brought his favourite camera down to the gallery, a Mamiya, he told her, a real man's camera because you needed man-sized hands to work it, although Annie Leibovitz used the same camera, he told her, as she had these man-sized hands. It was gratifying how everyone at the party last night was impressed by how Didi effortlessly worked her insider knowledge of Annie Leibovitz and this other sort-of-famous photographer and their Mamiyas into the conversation as she gamely offered her shorts as a hand towel, although the information was wasted on the butt-smacking guy from Ajax who thought Annie Leibovitz was *a stand-up comedian* and had never heard of the sort-of-famous photographer who took pictures of aging lady intellectuals and in fact had made a joke about lady intellectuals which she had thought was funny at the time, although she'd stopped laughing abruptly when she realized no one else found it funny and pretended that she was really just choking because her drink had gone down the wrong way. (No one thought to thump her on the back and later, much later, she couldn't help wondering what would've happened if she really had been choking.) After that came the incident with the palm tree and that Buddha-shirt girl, and waking up alone on the roof early this morning and climbing down into the apartment and peeking in on her hosts sleeping so peacefully in their bedroom, wrapped around each other, surrounded by old family photos in really nice-quality frames, and then letting herself out, but not before making a fair degree of noise in the bathroom hoping they'd wake up so she could wave goodbye and hear them tell her she'd been the life of the party.

Out on the balcony while the photographer flips the steaks, their fat hissing against the fake briquettes like a clique of fashionable viper-mouthed grade seven private-school girls,* and tells her about watching a bridge blow up outside of Sarajevo and how it was *too close for comfort* (emphasis his) and how a dog, a really ugly mutt, just stood on one side of this non-existent bridge whimpering and that all he wanted to

---

* Named Marnie, Teka, and Charlotte, names she's tried to forget for nine years now but which cling to her brainpan like the words *Deirdre fleas* gouged into the lip of a desk with the tip of a red Bic.

do was take a picture of the dog, not the bodies, and get out of there, Didi wonders whether it was maybe unwise to have hinted so broadly last night to everyone up there on the roof that Annie Leibovitz might be at this other party tonight at the photographer's place, which has turned out not to be a party of any kind at all.

Maybe it had been the soupy stillness of the air last night, the humidity that hung so thick the tiny pimento olive lights on the poor pissed-on palm tree glimmered as if through a fog, but she had felt as if there were a trampoline beneath her feet, felt as if anything could happen, so maybe she had convinced herself that Annie Leibovitz was going to be at the photographer's party, when, in fact, the photographer himself had quite possibly hinted at no such thing at all.

The telephone rings and rings again, but the photographer just ignores it, poking at those alarming potatoes with a fork and talking quietly, in this flat, even tone Didi associates with people who are going off their nut but straining to appear normal, about how no one seems to really listen anymore, how everyone is too busy "communicating" (he did the quote-mark thing with his fingers) to listen, and how there was a time when he flew to the direst places on earth to find pockets of silence so that he could hear himself think, and how, believe it or not, the deepest silences come in the aftermath of an explosion, in that thin wedge of time between the explosion itself and the chaos— the sirens and keening and yelling—that follows, and that this is the same no matter what country on earth you are in. And all the while he airdrops her name every few words like it's a relief package for starving Eritreans, *Believe it or not, Deirdre*, and *This is the same, Deirdre*, until she feels the skin tightening across her face, pulling her mouth into a grimace, although she's not sure if she should be smiling or nodding soberly.

Then there are her hands. She has absolutely no idea what to do with her hands, which are twitching to grab those two Zeppelin-sized potatoes and hurl them into the street like grenades. But then where would that leave her?

Last night had been so full of possibilities, even after she'd been forced to give up on the butt-smacking guy when that tight-T-shirted Buddha bitch came and stuck her tits in where they didn't belong. There'd been that Angelina Jolie–lipped VJ couple who looked like they could be brother and sister and who kept peering at her as if they were trying to convey something telepathically. Although that was before she tried to up her madcap quotient by juggling a handful of olives that went flying all over the place, causing that Eurasian tranny with the yellow hair and the five-inch cork-soled wedgies to slip on them and call her some choice names that weren't even worth repeating, after which a very pale woman with Smartie-coloured braces (who someone said was Rufus's new boyfriend's ex-girlfriend) raised her eyebrows at Didi in a seriously empathetic manner. Didi could practically see *You go, girl!* in a cartoon thought-bubble above the woman's head. Now, out here on the photographer's balcony, all this talk of explosions is bringing her down, bringing on the mortality thoughts, which are verboten, as her therapist has told her. Is this the old guy's way of making a play, of impressing her with his heroic journeys? Because if that's what he thinks, she's just not interested.

The photographer is looking at her as if it's her turn to say something. The barbecue tongs in his hand drip sauce out over the railing of the balcony and she wonders if somebody walking by in the morning fourteen storeys down below will think that what they see are drops of blood. And if somebody jumped off this balcony, naming no names, at this exact moment there would be a chalk outline down there tomorrow in the shape of a person as well as some real blood, which may or may not look as real to passersby as the drops of barbecue sauce. Didi considers telling the photographer this, thinks he may find it interesting, but instead she leans out over the railing and concentrates on looking as if she's peering so hard into the distance that she can divine the future, when in fact she can't see anything at all through the haze of barbecue smoke and the pinpricks of static dancing behind her eyes.

In the photographer's bedroom, after inspecting the disappointingly dull contents of his bathroom medicine cabinet, Didi flings open the closet and sees an ocean of shirts, all in pale blue denim. She hugs the shirts to her and burrows her face into them as if she were his long-time lover missing him dreadfully while he was off on assignment somewhere remote and squalid, and she thinks that if he were to wander in at this exact moment to find out what was taking her so long, his heart would involuntarily contract at the sight of a young woman so capable of devotion that she's transported from her earthly surroundings.

Didi deeply inhales a scent she finds surprisingly fresh for a man his age, a scent that scurries up her nostrils like the first sharp tang of spring, until she realizes it's the smell of dry-cleaned clothes, and because she's allergic to dry-cleaning chemicals she knows it's only a matter of time before her eyelids start swelling shut and her nose begins to run and then any chance at all for salvaging the evening will be gone. Back in the bathroom she checks her face, which still seems all right, although she has to close one eye and then the other in order to focus properly. She thought she was a redhead this week, but the person staring back at Didi has this black hair and these terrible chunky bangs. When did she dye her hair black?

When did she have it cut? This whole time she's been acting like a redhead, doing red-headed things with her hands, saying red-headed things, trying to think red-headed thoughts, and her hair has been black? Was it black last night?

She's already back in the dining room refilling her glass when she remembers she didn't flush, unlike early this morning when, after waking up alone on the roof (even the palm tree was gone!) and somehow managing to crawl down into the apartment before being sick, Didi made sure she flushed and then flushed again. Then she'd washed her face, scraping at the flecks of roof pitch with an AirMiles card someone had left in the soap dish, before stepping into the hallway and belting out the theme song from *The Mary Tyler Moore Show*. One of her hosts appeared in the doorway of the bedroom, wide-eyed, naked, just as she was pretending to toss her hat into the air Mary Richards–style, and closed the door in her face, loudly, but she caught the pretend hat anyway just to prove she didn't need other people around to have fun.

It was only afterwards, when she was standing down on Adelaide, that she realized she didn't have cab fare or even enough for the streetcar and had to walk all the way home while flipping the bird at ignorant would-be johns in rusting Impalas and gleaming Isuzu Rodeos with bicycle racks on the back who couldn't differentiate if their very lives depended on it between her ironically short terry-cloth shorts (that had just been at a party with Rufus Wainwright and his new lover and the latter's understanding and rather empathetic ex-girlfriend) and something a hooker would wear. And after all that she had so looked forward to tonight, to a fun evening in a fourteenth-floor luxury apartment belonging to a semi-famous photographer who specialized in portraits of aging women intellectuals, *so excuse her!*

The steaks and those very large, scary baked potatoes have somehow made their way onto the table and she finds herself sitting in front of a plate with a knife and fork in her hands and the photographer is still talking, something about how if he hadn't become a photographer he would've been a short-order cook, an excellent short-order cook, because that's how much he likes a *well-greased grill* (??!!), and how much simpler his life would've been, and Didi wonders why he's telling her these things, wonders if he maybe has her confused with somebody else, with this Deirdre whose name he keeps snapping his jaws down on as if they're a leghold trap, because, well, explosions, if you like that kind of thing, could be considered a turn-on, but a well-greased grill can't be construed as anything other than a well-greased grill.

In between all his words, if she squints, she can see that he's trying to tell her something and that it has nothing to do with innuendo. She knows she should be interested in these things he's talking about, that somehow these things matter, but she isn't. In fact, they make her feel itchy.

What she really, really wants to ask, once and for all, is *What are we doing here?* She tries to will this simple question into being, to thrust it into the air between them like a magician conjuring a dove from the old-fashioned beige clutch purse of the mousy divorcee in the front row, the bird's small breast throbbing against the magician's thumb, the woman feeling off-balance but delighted (*He picked me!*), but when the words refuse to materialize, Didi tugs her blouse off over her head and lets it float to the floor.

The place had looked spotless, but now she sees dust scudding in drifts over the dulled parquet like clouds as the blouse wafts down in slow motion. In these elongated seconds, between her shirt coming off and him looking up from his plate and noticing, Didi has time to think she should be happy because here she is just one degree of separation from Annie Leibovitz and, in effect, only two degrees of separation from John and Yoko, David Byrne, Chris Rock, Nicole, Brad, Ben, Gwyneth, Kate—from *everybody*. This should make her feel elated, but instead she's filled with this prickly, fur-bearing sadness. She is, after all, only one degree of separation from that ugly dog at the edge of that bridge that no longer exists, in a country that no longer exists—so close that she could be that ugly dog, and in fact, if you looked closely enough, she is that ugly dog, and she needs to know if that dog ever jumped into the river to try to get to the other side or if he's still there shivering and whimpering for his owners, for the only people who loved him no matter what and who may or may not exist anymore anywhere on earth.

SOMEONE IS KILLING THE GREAT MOTIVATIONAL SPEAKERS OF AMERIKA

I've stopped caring about skeptics, but if they libel or defame me they will end up in court.
—URI GELLER, PSYCHIC SPOON BENDER

Belief is commonly easier to acquire and maintain than knowledge.
—BARRETT L. DORKO, P.T.

You try telling that to Dodge.
—ME

Someone is killing the great motivational speakers of Amerika and I am afraid I may be next. In an effort not to alarm my followers, I have camouflaged my disappearance as a wilderness retreat. The surroundings are more rustic than we are accustomed to and there have been grumblings about the lack of facilities. I tell them their ancestors didn't have backpacks containing rolls of three-ply toilet paper and antibacterial wipes; they had to make do with leaves and corn husks. In more recent times, it's possible they resorted to sections of newspapers that left their backsides inked with the TSE Composite Index or *Blondie*. Soon everyone is enthusiastically gathering foliage, although Dodge, twiddling his small goatee, complains about not having a copy of the latest *Vancouver Sun* editorial page. Dodge, with his almost indiscernible sense of humour, has for a long time now caused me equal measures of joy and grief.

As I watch my crew milling about with purpose—collecting firewood, securing tarps, taking inventory of the granola bars and shrink-wrapped Bavarian rye breads, the nut butters and fruit leathers, giving each other a hand—I can see it has been worth it. Is this not all I ever wanted? Cinders unfolds a foil astronaut blanket and wraps it around my shoulders. Felix has torn up a patch of moss he now cradles in his arms like a kitten. He advises me to stroke it with a pinky finger while keeping my eyes screwed shut tight. Gratitude wells in my breasts for all I have wrought. If this isn't synergy, what is?

Campfire songs are suggested, and I don't see why not. We are too isolated for anyone to hear us. And it is very late. The moon is a high, hard rind through sweating cedars. Hives prickle my neck from all the fungi around. The city is far away, only the occasional magnesium flare through hemlock and Douglas fir. Something in our small fire cracks like a pistol shot. *I'm a bow-legged chicken, I'm a knock-kneed hen*, Felix sings, his lisp almost indistinct, and the rest join in, even The Kevster, who during the past few weeks has taken to lurking on the perimeters with a sneer perma-pressed onto his face. *Never bin so happy since I don't know when*. Except for Pudding, who stares at the sky, as always, as if waiting for a signal.

Pudding is the only one I've never been able to get through to.

My troubles began almost a year ago, with the publication of an obscure scientific document, a paper rife with antiquated language and reactionary ideas (the lingua franca of *fear*). Science is on thin ground these days and particle physicists were up in arms: "[We're] damned if we're going to stand by and let a handful of rogue advocates of quantum quackery overrun quantum mechanics, a field of research that could lead, finally, to a Theory of Everything" (Brisbane Convention Report, 2011, p. iv).

Snake oil was mentioned. The phrase *half-baked* was deployed. *String theory* was draped around the text like rolls of crepe paper livening up a fiftieth-anniversary party.

You would have been hard pressed to even find a mention of the report online until a Danish newspaper ran an inflammatory series of editorial cartoons on the "debate." Deepak Chopra shoving a Dr. Seussian Schrödinger's cat into a microwave oven. Anthony Robbins® putting it "doggie style" to physicist Niels Bohr, who knelt on a bed of burning coals. Uri Geller dining on Einstein's entrails à la *The Cook, the Thief, His Wife, and Her Lover* using a large bent spoon. Esoteric "European" humour at its worst.

But the Internet being what it is, the gist of the argument was soon translated into Amerikan. It was at that point that things took a turn for the worse.

Our belief in human energy fields, in mind-over-matter responses to our increasing health problems, threatened not only the physicists but those in the field of conventional medicine. Powerful alliances were formed.* They unfortunately had, *have*, an erroneous understanding of bioenergetics: "The belief that human consciousness controls reality," the scientists scoffed. *Control*s is a misnomer. *Manipulates* is closer; *defines* would be more accurate.

Was it altogether too simple-minded of me to ask: *Why can't we just get along?* ("What the Heck?" promotional brochure, March 2012.) Apparently so. Because it was soon afterwards that the death threats began.

Dodge has brought his girlfriend with him. I'm not convinced this was a good idea. Sam is a slippery one, very all-Amerikan in her locution, *yes ma'am, absolutely ma'am*, and with a look on her face some may describe as beatific, but that strikes me as bland. Her energy field is like a clear-cut, with no remaining signs of life, not even a termite.

She sits in a patch of sun filtered through fern and cedar, telling Felix a story, the light glinting off her wedding finger, Dodge hovering around them like some kind of manservant. She wears what is called a "purity ring" and has persuaded Dodge to wear one as well. To put it bluntly, the rings are a symbol of sexual abstinence, although Sam didn't put it that way. She just held it up in front of my face and said, "True love waits." Then she patiently told me, as if I were a small child, that it was a reminder of the commitment she had made to God to remain pure until marriage. I should be relieved, but somehow I find this offensive. Isn't Dodge good enough for

---

* I hesitate to indict pharmaceutical concerns, as prescriptions for citalopram, my birth control pill, Alesse, as well as my Ventolin inhaler have kept me afloat for more years than I care to tally. I have always held that the existence (and acceptance) of "grey areas" makes us more human, although this is a point of view that is best kept to yourself if you are going to succeed as a motivational speaker in Amerika.

her? Is this what constitutes sex education in Amerika today?

So much hard work over the years, so many appearances made while hopped up on antihistamines or fighting rogue waves of menstrual cramps, scalp itchy with excess sebum, wondering when I last had the opportunity to take a shower. Did I ever let on that I was suffering? You succeed through *terrorizing the negative impulse* (*My Emotional Fatwa*, Golden Agouti Press, 2009, p. 64). This is, I contend, because you're never going to stop the rain by whinging.*

I clap my hands and announce that it's time for our daily Pronouncements. Time to break up this little idyll.

The word *pure* really irks me. "Gets my tits in a knot, Alice," as my friend Ingrid would say.

We sit cross-legged in a semicircle. A bird demonically shrills somewhere in the forest canopy. "I am striving to overcome the urge to snog Sam until my lips fall off," pronounces Dodge.†
The Kevster makes a rude noise, and Sam covers her face with her purity-ring hand.

"That is so *not* a serious Pronouncement," says Cinders. She is the follower who has taken my teachings most to heart. The Kevster likes to refer to her as Rulebook.

"I am striving to stop eating so many high-fructose, high-glucose snack foods," says Cinders, who struggles with body image. During Pronouncements we are meant to pledge to overcome something standing in the way of our future happiness.

---

* To paraphrase the great Amerikan songwriter Hal David.

† Dodge adopted this Briticism after reading the Harry Potter series several years back (the characters he identified most closely with were Fred and George Weasley). Whether this is an affectation versus a general affection for the term is impossible to say. This is Dodge, after all.

"I am striving to overcome doubt," says Sam, somewhat cryptically in my opinion, but I don't ask, "Doubt about what?" You could say that I am striving to be a more tolerant person.

Sam is older than Dodge by about six years. Technically, at nineteen, he is still a teenager, although legally speaking she cannot be accused of robbing the cradle. Still, there is a way I have found her looking at me at times, woman-to-woman you could call it, that is unsettling.

"I am striving to control my bladder at night so I can have a sleepover at Dexter's place when we get home," says Felix. I grant him an encouraging wink. Felix is reassuringly goal-oriented. That we may not be going home anytime soon would not be useful information to impart to him at this point.

The Kevster remains silent. Pudding as well, but that goes without saying.

The worst accusation from the scientists, on a personal level, was that we were "confusing bioenergetic fields with the ether."

If our energy fields don't exist—what is this? This luminous face turned skyward, pale irises, the flecks in them wildly kaleidoscopic, her skin, that way of looking. Pudding has such an intense aura. There are times I have witnessed static crackling blue from her scalp, her fine hair rising and quavering like the tentacles of a sea anemone. It is as if she is communing with the unseen particles in the air around us, decoding them into her private language somewhere deep in her hermit kingdom, in her Arkadia.

I have far from given up on what quantum mind theory may be able to do for Pudding. In the TRIUMF cyclotron, the gigantic particle accelerator at the university, various matters and antimatters collide to release pure energy in the form of gamma rays. The subatomic particles travel in the accelerator in a spiral, and a spiral is the primary geometric form in which thought waves travel. If we could get within shouting distance of these gamma rays and direct them to interact with Pudding's already overactive energy field, perhaps they could unlock her from inside her private realm.* The radiation issue remains unresolved. But it is a risk I'm willing to take.

Our location in this particular arboreal area, then, in the vicinity of the university's research facility, is not entirely without foresight. Somewhere farther from the city would have been safer, but *if you're convinced the tortoise will lose to the hare, then what is the point of the race?*† (*Five Fables for the Future*, Golden Agouti Press, 2011, p. 109.)

Infiltrating the TRIUMF cyclotron has become my number one priority. For far too long has Pudding remained on the periphery—a cipher, a "changeling," as people like her were called in the past. It is my duty to bring Pudding fully into the fold. I have that can-do feeling surging through me, despite the furtive whisperings between Dodge and his virgin concubine and The Kevster's surly and penetrating silence.

It is time to admit what we have become. A rebel unit. No longer on the run, but proactive. To think that I almost succumbed to despair when I first perceived that my life was in danger. My followers give me strength even in their own moments of weakness. My platoon. I like the sound of that. *Ten-hut!*

I must find a way to polish my boots.

---

* There is also an application called positron emission tomography. (I prefer the more anthropomorphic PET, as, apparently, do the researchers themselves.) PET allows for a true scan of a living human brain at work. A scientific euphemism for "mind reading"?
† I am not averse to a little borrowing here and there from the classics of literature. Browning is a particular favourite. As for Aesop, what is there not to love?

Tony Robbins was the first of us to disappear. Initially, a publicity stunt was suspected, but for a man of his voracious public appetite to voluntarily remain out of the limelight for so long seemed unfathomable. His financial holdings and current and former wives and associates were investigated, his accounts frozen. It has been eight months now and a body has yet to be recovered. A few months after his disappearance, Zachariah Madoff and Bernie "Hola!" Rodriguez were found dead within days of each other. The cause of death in both cases was eventually attributed to natural causes. (Who but scientists, *international* scientists, I ask, could cover their tracks like that, mimicking a coronary embolus and a subarachnoid hemorrhage so effectively as to dupe two coroners at the top of their game?) Werner Washington died more publicly, shot by a sniper at a shareholders' meeting in the Houston Astrodome. (The laughable lone-gunman theory has been widely debunked but continues to be the FBI's official line.)

Deepak now travels Kevlar-coated, with two armed guards, in an electric vehicle reminiscent of the Popemobile. He remains mum about whether he's received death threats, but the security at his residences and events rivals that of the phalanx of sharp-shooters and the bulletproof glass dome at Amerikan President Obama's second inauguration.*

I was closer to Tony than most people would care to acknowledge.† I have had night visions in which his baseball-glove-sized hands are cradling my head and his teeth are lighting a path through the darkness. In truth, darkness is

---

* It is an ugly world out there for the truth-seekers and soothsayers among us. For those with the instinct for conciliation, punishment comes swift and hard, as we have so sadly witnessed.
† Including his third wife.

something I have never feared. I have the eyes of a cat. I have little use for Tony's glowing teeth, but could use some of his advice right about now. I simply try not to even think about his hands.

We have managed to move closer to the TRIUMF facility, undetected but for the occasional raccoon and the unseen birds that twitter and caw their way across the forest canopy. After studying the diagrams of the site I obtained from the Internet, it has become obvious to me that breaching the inner sanctum will be trickier than I thought: the cyclotron is situated three storeys beneath the ground and is shielded by triplicate layers of 100-tonne concrete blocks, each 4.5 metres thick.

There is, of course, the recourse to a public tour* to gain entry and then staging a distraction while I spirit Pudding nearer the chamber. I can practically hear my friend Ingrid, who is an excellent slam poet, spit, "Permission is for losers."† Besides, I am a wanted woman.

The security, though, is not what I had assumed. The sprawling and tastefully landscaped site comprises several buildings without, if the diagrams are to be believed, fibre optic security or even electrified fencing around the perimeter. An invitation to a reckoning.

This mission gives me a feeling of liberation I have not felt in a long time. The big question now is: *Do I share the details of my plan? Or do we proceed on a need-to-know basis?* My attempts at a military style of discipline have been met with a degree of resistance. After so many years of establishing my

---

* Wednesdays and Fridays at 1 P.M. Prior booking recommended.
† I plan to include this line in my next book, with permission, of course.

authority, I perceive a growing slackness among my followers that bespeaks, if not quite insurrection, then some form of unconscious revolt.

Sam sits astride a cedar log massaging Dodge's shaved scalp as if it's a crystal ball and she's divining the future. What does she see? Herself and Dodge surrounded by the emaciated children of an orphanage in Chad or Pune, or by bald little babies of their own in a stucco fourplex in East Vancouver? Is that a path to happiness for either of them?

"Velcro. There's an example," Dodge says. "Think of burrs sticking to a dog's belly fur. Think of the entire planet as a humungous R&D lab. There are sustainable air-conditioned buildings inspired by the study of termite mounds, wind turbines based on the humpback whale's fin." Dodge, it seems, intends to study biomimicry. This is not something we have had time to discuss. Much like the Sam liaison.

"Would God approve?" Sam wonders out loud. She doesn't appear to require an answer from Dodge, who just closes his eyes and sighs with pleasure against the circling pressure of her fingers. What about me? What if I don't approve of his misplaced faith in science?

Why does no one think to offer me a massage?

Cinders wants to know what I'm going to do about the cougar The Kevster has spotted. They never used to question, especially Cinders. I would say jump and Cinders would ask, "Horizontal or vertical?" (*You're O.K.—I'm K2*, Golden Agouti Press, 2010, p. 156.) Now it's become all why, what, when? Perhaps the anomie that has been creeping through the general population has gone viral, infiltrating the spores of the various fungi that proliferate here and compromising the morale of my troops.

Need I say, look it in the eye and show it who is boss? Need I say, winners are not eaten? Winners bite, chew, and disgorge what they don't need. I learned this lesson from a boy cousin what seems like an eternity ago now. We had been arguing about who was the real creative genius, Elton John or Bernie Taupin.* He tore my cherished poster of "The Desiderata," designed to evoke an illuminated manuscript, from my bedroom wall and crammed it into his mouth piece by piece, gnashing ferociously. When he was done, only a gummy strip with the words Go placidly amid the noise and has— hung from one of his incisors. Above my desk the Hang in There, Baby! poster curled upward from the wall, masking tape in petrified clumps, a Siamese cat clinging to a telephone wire with a frenzied look on its face. "Eat or be eaten," my cousin growled. "Kill or be killed."

Ricky had what you would call charisma. But he didn't enjoy what you'd call a successful adulthood.

Cinders has wet herself rather than dare venture outside of our little enclave. I think we're long past due for a visualization circle.

There was a time, back in high school, when I would have described myself as a Christian Existentialist. A believer in God, albeit one who believed not in personal destiny, but rather in personal responsibility. I was a somewhat gloomy girl who

---

* You may ask, whatever happened to Bernie Taupin? In 2006 he won a Golden Globe for his song "A Love That Will Never Grow Old" for the film Brokeback Mountain. In early 2012 he collaborated once again with Elton John to write the song commemorating HRH Prince Charles's long overdue ascension to the British throne, "Midnight in the Kingdom." Bernie Taupin has been married four times and is the proud owner of a bucking bull used in professional competition in Amerika. If pressed, I will admit to still carrying a small flame for him.

wept during the singing of "Kumbaya" at school assemblies.*
Our Catholic school was remarkably progressive, thanks
to Vatican II. It was through a lanky, good-natured religion
teacher that I discovered *Zen and the Art of Motorcycle
Maintenance*, and Carlos Castaneda and his *Teachings of
Don Juan*. It is to Mr. S. and to Cousin Ricky that I owe my
metaphysical awakening.

We hold hands, because there is nothing equivalent to the
holding of hands to pass on currents of self-generated electricity
and intensify our energy fields. I sense that placid Sam may be a
weak link. Pudding, on the other hand, standing between Felix
and me, has a charge that could fire up a fleet of cross-Strait
hydrofoils.

There is a strong wind sweeping across the tops of the trees;
I hear it rather than feel it. More than a whisper, less than a
roar. And a smell settling in not unlike that of a cabin that has
been closed up for the winter. It emanates from our little group,
a reminder that none of us have bathed for almost a week.

"I'm thinking about nachos with the works," says Dodge,
"the kind they have at Tinseltown in that flimsy cardboard
dish with the melted cheese product bubbling like lava." When
his eyes are closed it's easy to imagine Dodge is still a child,
filled with wayward charm and bereft of the flinty humour. It
is impossible to tell if he is being genuine, but as no one starts
giggling we move on.

"I'm thinking about a handheld electronic device," Felix
says, his lisp prominent and endearing, at odds with his preternaturally advanced vocabulary. "Even an old Nintendo DS."

---

* My arduous journey from pessimist to optimist is described in detail in *My Emotional
Fatwa*.

"That's the spirit," I say. I had forbidden anyone to bring a cellphone or nano—to preserve the purity of the retreat, I told them. If the new President of Amerika is forced to survive without her BlackBerry for security purposes, then so can I.

Cinders says, "I'm thinking about Pudding saying her first word. I'm thinking it should be, 'Howdy, Pardners!'" Cinders has a thing for cowboys, which I'm not sure is age appropriate. She opens her eyes and looks at me, and I give her an encouraging smile and squeeze Pudding's hand. Technically speaking, my eyes shouldn't have been open either, but chances are good Cinders will not broadcast my flouting of the rules. "That's two words," says Felix.

Even Sam seems game, although typically opaque. "I'm thinking about a dark path easily traversed." I cannot help but admire her correct usage of *traversed*. For someone I have never seen poking her button nose into a book, she is very well-spoken.

It's all going so nicely when The Kevster plops down onto his butt and leans back on his elbows, legs splayed. When did his legs get so long? "I want Dad." He draws it out so it sounds like *Duh-ad*.

Do I say, "Was it Dad who stayed up for nights on end rubbing your back in soothing circles as you writhed with night terrors brought on from DVDs you know you shouldn't have watched at Calvin's house?" (The *mole people*! I never could understand what could have been so terrifying about the mole people.) Do I say, "Was it Dad who drove out to every cheap-plastic-off-gassing Walmart in the Lower Mainland in monsoon rains because you had to have a Dark Knight costume?" Do I say, "Do you think *Duh-ad* gives a shit?"

To my credit I merely drop Pudding's hand and shake off Felix's sticky grip and walk off in the direction of the unseen coastline. The ocean is out there. Somewhere beyond this increasingly oppressive foliage and the gnarled trunks, these optimistic nurse logs and fecund mulches, is the edge of Amerika and beyond that the rest of the world. It has been a very long while since I've felt anything approaching the sting of tears. Now is not the time to succumb to a pitiful nostalgia. But, unbidden, "Buffalo Springfield Again"* rises from somewhere inside me.

I was once young and I was wild—but refused to let it eat me up.

Winners are not sentimental. Winners look forward, not back. And still, the tears begin to fall.

It rained all night. Rapping against the tarps, weighing them down in deep troughs, the water cascading off like minor Niagaras. The ground surrounding us is now marshland. It's that squelching kind of weather that is counterproductive to a sense of esprit de corps. But at least the rain has tamped down the effects of the fungal spores and my head feels clear.

I awoke this morning with a strong feeling that Sam has a gun. Why would Sam have a gun? Did I dream it? Did I see it?

Everyone else is still sleeping, so perhaps it is not yet morning. With this greyness it's difficult to tell when day begins.

Of all the shocks over the past few months, I would have to say that the one that had me reeling was the loss of Viva Sawatsky. Lively little Viva who broke through the gender barrier in our field back when most of us were still busy daring each other to lift pots of green-apple-scented lip gloss from drugstore cosmetics displays.

---

* I greatly admire the great Amerikan singer-songwriter Neil Young but have often wondered whether it would hurt him to try doing something with his hair.

How old would she have been? Well over seventy, maybe even over eighty. She never did divulge her age. She was found slumped in the green room of NBC's Alameda Ave. studios minutes before she was to appear on the *new* new Conan O'Brien to talk about her latest (and now final) book, *87 Ways to Plug into the Power of Whimsy*. Her premise, which I am not certain I fully appreciate the brilliance of yet, was that there is an area of the brain that is exclusively wired for whimsy and yet only 0.000000087 percent of the total world population has the preternatural ability to tap into its power. Clothing designer Betsey Johnson is one of these people. Idi Amin was another.* And, of course, Viva herself.

Since when are *Tonight Show* guests left unattended? The story is that Viva sent her publicist out for a fish taquito and then choked to death on a misdirected swallow of Ensure. But where were the Conan O'Brien people? Why the absence of other guests in the green room? It bears mentioning that the head of Molecular Biologists Without Borders had been slated to be on that night and had been bumped at the eleventh hour for Viva.

If her, then why not me? That's what I couldn't stop asking myself.

It's all about the cougar now. Its yellow eyes. Its liquid haunches. Its propensity to be there even when it's not. My platoon is preoccupied with peripheral vision. I appear to have a rebellion on my hands. The rebels are rebelling. They keep the fire going day and night, undeterred by my admonishments that we could be found out. I believe rangers are now patrolling these lands.

---

* According to Viva, whimsy itself is neutral. The user is the determinant of whether it has a "creative" or "destructive" charge.

The cougar is afraid of fire, they insist. This "fact" is no doubt a vestigial memory from Walt Disney's *Jungle Book* or an episode of *Kratts' Creatures*. But a mountain lion is not a tiger despite their shared DNA, just as *a goat is not a yak no matter how similar their milk may taste* (ibid.).

Did The Kevster really see the beast? This would not be the first time he has lied with such conviction.

No, Sam could not have a gun. But neither was it a dream.

We are now camped right outside the TRIUMF facility, obscured by a screen of trees. I would send someone for reconnaissance, but even Dodge refuses to leave the circle around the campfire, not out of fear in his case, I imagine, but out of a sense of fraternal duty. He's gone commando, one of Sam's scarves wrapped around his waist like a sarong. You might think this look would compromise his ability to gain the trust of the others, but they have begun to listen to Dodge with a puppy-like intentness. Even The Kevster. My own sense of authority has begun to seep from me like pus from a weeping wound.* We have had no Pronouncements for days, no sense of striving. It is as if they are willing to throw away the chance for future happiness in exchange for a false sense of security in the moment.

The cyclotron is thrumming in the near distance. It's like the murmuring of a large crowd before the speaker comes on, the swell of anticipation. But is it even possible to hear the sound from so far underneath the earth? Or is it simply vibrating the very ground we occupy? I find I can't distinguish it from the motor of my own heart.

---

* It is not that I seek to liken myself to Christ on the cross but at times the looks I get from Dodge are as piercing as the point of St. Longinus's lance.

The fire-walking cannot be put off any longer. The charcoal briquettes I have hauled from campsite to campsite, without complaint, form a narrow path that extends over at least three metres. A little fire starter splashed here and there and a few clicks of my butane BBQ lighter and it will soon be glowing with red-hot embers, the air rippled with the rising heat. Although I have been planning this for a long time, I have never practised. Fire-walking is not a thing to be achieved in private, if it is to be achieved at all.

A small dog darts into our clearing, chases its tail, and barks. Its owner hails it from the distance: "Toto! Toto!" And just as quickly it is gone, but not before Pudding turns from where she is arranging pine cones into categories based on her mysterious aesthetic criteria and extends a hand towards the dog. Pudding extends a hand! It takes me a moment or two to collect myself.

With my boots and socks off and my pants rolled up, I am dismayed by my stubbled white legs and neglected toenails. Surprised as well, as if these sad specimens belong to some other woman. Sam glances at me in that way she has of looking without seeming to look. Well, feast away, young lady. Someday all this will be yours!

There are those who would choose to tell you that our skin is a poor conductor of heat, as are coals covered with ash, and that therefore walking across them is no different from quickly pressing your fingers to a loaf of banana bread baking in the oven in order to test for doneness.* I prefer to undertake this,

---

* Other scientific detractors cite the Leidenfrost effect (as musical as it sounds, it's a dispiriting explanation of the phenomenon of fire-walking). In effect, just as drops of water dance about on a hot skillet because of the protective layer of vapour formed by evaporation, a fire-walker's inevitably sweaty feet help create a similar protective layer.

my first fire-walk ever, with the same spirit of humility that motivates the young girls on the island of Bali to traverse fire unaided but for their belief in benevolent gods.*†‡

All these years of talking like a winner. At last I *will be* a winner.

I look over at The Kevster, his face strangled. "Would *Duh-ad* walk through fire for you?" I point at Sam, who is braiding Cinders's hair, Cinders between her knees, head lowered, not looking at me, and ask Dodge, "Would *she* walk through fire for you?"

He doesn't answer, just sits down in his makeshift sarong and pulls off his sneakers and then his socks, flinging them aside. His feet are long and smooth like his father's. Jesus feet. There are small tufts of hair on what he used to call his foot knuckles.

Dodge steps towards the smouldering coals, and for a moment I fear I have made a terrible mistake. His arms held out from his sides, like a small boy pretending to fly, he strides quickly. The fringe on the scarf curls against the heat. Sam and the children suck in their breath, all except Pudding, who scans the sky, perhaps reading something in the contrail of the jet that passed overhead minutes ago, forever ago now—bound for Tokyo or Hong Kong or Sydney. Dodge makes it to the end and lurches onto the forest floor as if stepping off a fast-moving escalator. He hasn't uttered a sound.

---

* In 2002, twenty Australian Kentucky Fried Chicken outlet managers had to be treated for burns caused by fire-walking. I ask you, is the Leidenfrost effect substantially different Down Under, or is it that they were insufficiently motivated in mind and spirit?
† My colleague Tolly Burkan has called fire-walking a metaphor and contends that if you can master it, you can also muster the courage to demand a raise. With all due respect, this diminishes all of us, does it not?
‡ Some useful advice from Tony Robbins: Visualize walking the coals while chanting, "Cool moss, cool moss, cool moss."

"That's love, Dodge," I say, clapping my hands in a weak approximation of girlish glee, that's how giddy I feel. "That's faith." Relieved that we have arrived at this. Finally. I almost salute him. In fact, I quell the urge to crush him in my arms in an enormous hug, something I haven't done for a long time.

"No, *mother*." He practically ejects the words as if they're spent bullets. "That's science."

I have no time to process this because Cinders is screaming. Pudding holds a briquette in her hand, no pain on her face, but there is the smell of burning flesh. The Kevster is the one who pries it from her fingers while Sam hurtles to retrieve the first-aid kit. I find myself unable to move, fixated on the scrim of heat rising off the briquettes and wondering if I should still try to walk through fire.

When Dodge was born he had more hair than he does now. What a thing to remember. But I do remember. I can recall each of their births with a startling clarity; the exquisitely searing pain infused with jaw-clenching joy. Now Pudding is keening. The first sound she has ever made.

Pushing Sam and Dodge aside, I reach for my daughter.

I wake to the shrill cry of a bald eagle. How could I have slept so soundly, like a dead woman? The last thing I remember is holding Pudding's bandaged hand to my breast and closing my eyes while the others either wept or whispered around me. And beneath us the eternal come-hither thrum of the cyclotron.

But even the cyclotron is silent this morning. The campfire doused. Camp broken. Is that how they put it? Or struck? The camp has been struck, that is a fact, as if by a smart bomb. There is no Pudding, no Cinders, no Felix, no Kevster, no Sam.

Dodge has taken them all away. Is this weakness or responsibility?

There are things I could do. I could stride through the forest in a shambolic rage, uprooting hemlocks and sharpening my teeth on towering cedars, bearing down on small animals. I could stalk that cougar, mount it and ride it back into the city, gather my followers and march on the towers of the faithless, with burning coals in the pouches of my cheeks, spitting fire.

But who am I without my platoon, without my flesh and blood?

The punchline of a joke?

A woman walking across burning coals to get to the other side.

MISTER KAKAMI

The man who is in charge of ruining Patrick Kakami's life prowls the halls of Vancouver's Telefilm office in search of personnel.

Across the street in Victory Square, rats the size of Whiskas-fed house cats patrol the base of the war memorial for abandoned pizza crusts and dropped panini fillings. In the garbage-strewn alley below the funding agency's boardroom window, a seventeen-year-old heroin addict is in the final throes of an overdose, telescoping pupils in bruised eyes like some wide-eyed child in a velvet painting by a direct descendant of Bosch.

Inside, the workstations are alive with screen savers and nothing else—undulating seaweed, someone's diaper-clad toddler, Bart Simpson on a skateboard flipping the bird. Syd Gross leafs through a bulging manila file folder labelled FUBAR, thinking, *I'll say.*

Syd hates these trips to the West Coast. You can't get a decent veal sandwich and just yesterday he met a woman who lived on a houseboat in False Creek who gave her two Abyssinian kittens bimonthly fish-oil enemas. Guys walked around downtown carrying waterproof briefcases and wearing flip-flops. How could you do business with these people when their hair-tufted toes were showing? It was like negotiating with hobbits. One of the teamsters on the Vancouver segment of the *Rain Dog* shoot, a soft, fiftyish man in an *April Wine 4-Ever!* T-shirt and Teva sandals whose job it was to drive in the honey wagon each day and then sit there for twelve hours doing absolutely sweet fuck all (for $37.46 an hour), kept telling anyone within earshot, "I came back from Hollyhock feeling spiritually replenished." *Get a real job*, Syd thought. *Get a pair of real shoes.*

From a cubicle in the far corner of the large open-air office, Syd hears the kind of gulping for breath children engage in when words fail them. He finds a man around his own age, mid-forties, sporting shocking sideburns and Tweety Bird suspenders, sitting on the ground crying, hunched over a mound of photocopied scripts, a clutch of forms strewn around him. The man looks up at Syd. "I spent the whole night at Kinko's"—he pauses, striving to get his voice under control— "and I still missed the phase-three script-development funding deadline." Syd makes a clucking sound with his tongue.

Because the thing about Sydney Gross is this. His name, his manner, his voice, his deep regard for the bottom line and affinity for darkened rooms redolent of the smell of Golden Topping® may have predestined him to become a producer of moving pictures, but somewhere along his ribbon of DNA there's a den-mother gene programmed to respond to sorrow. This is the reason he continues to champion Patrick Kakami, not because the guy is on top of his game, but because Syd can sense he's unravelling. And this is the reason Syd lowers himself onto the faux-distressed concrete floor, in his $475 (plus GST) "sport" slacks from Harry Rosen, and allows this weeping man, this complete stranger, to lay his head on his shoulder as he gives the man a one-armed hug.

Above them, a vulcanized-rubber wide-mouth bass mounted on the wall begins to move its tail and sing, in a deep, Barry White–type voice: "Take me to the river, / Drop me in the water ..."

Syd's cellphone jangles in his breast pocket, the *Chariots of Fire* ring tone more cloying than triumphant.

"What do you mean he's disappeared?" Syd hears himself squawking, his shirt front damp with another man's tears. He hates the squawk. But there's nothing to be done for it—it makes guest appearances when he's over-agitated, like acid reflux. "There's no transport off the island till Sunday. He can't just disappear."

The rubber fish, oblivious to the drama on either end of the phone, continues to sing. Something about oceans. Something about love.

"Mr. Kakami? Mr. Kakami!" The first AD, a wraithlike woman from South Africa who always used the honorific and looked like a Brontë scholar, floated into Patrick's field of vision. They were four scenes behind and it wasn't even noon. Patrick summoned his trademark look of benign concern and huddled over her rain-pocked copy of the shooting script, randomly scratching out shots that, a few weeks ago, he would've sacrificed his right testicle to keep. She was clearly relieved, yet continued to look at him as if he were a man who kept his first wife in the attic. What he was, in fact, was a man struggling to remember why he was here in this island rainforest, surrounded by all this slurry of activity, in the first place.

Because. Because the low hum of his parents' voices, whenever he had drifted off to sleep in the back seat of the car on the way home from the movie theatre, was the greatest soundtrack ever made. Because, once upon a time, Jessica Lange's face had been the closest thing to looking straight into the sun and not going blind. Because his mother had always cheered at the end of that scene in *The Sound of Music* where the nuns stole the distributor cap from the Nazis' car. Because, at eight, he'd developed a heart condition (sluggish flow through left ventricle) and his mother, afraid he'd die in his sleep, let him stay awake many nights in the long weeks leading up to the operation (experimental at the time, routine today), his head in her lap as the blue light of late-night movies on the oldies channel flickered over them (how his mother had adored Ernest Borgnine in *Marty* and Sidney Poitier in *Lilies of the Field*—again, those nuns!) *but don't tell your father*, her unexpectedly cool finger to his lips.

Because his own childhood had once seemed endless— something he's thought about a great deal ever since overhearing that story on the ferry, perhaps apocryphal, about the nameless toddler who'd speed-dialed 911 on his father's cellphone, obliviously, and even gleefully, ending his childhood as he knew it.

Because he had once been a child who was unconditionally loved and cherished, Patrick Kakami had been in a hurry to grow up and make what amounted to the world's most perfect movie—the cinematic equivalent of a mother's breath in a son's ear at three-thirty in the morning.

A moving picture so sublime the intended viewer's heart would fold in on itself in an origami of joy.

And now? Now Patrick was *going through the motions*— wind up the little art-house director and watch him make a film! How had he ended up making *films* and not movies, when it was good old-fashioned flicks, middlebrow and sentimental, excluding only those who didn't believe in magic, that he so loved? When had he turned from snub-nosed, red-headed Paddy K. into "artfully stubble-headed auteur Patrick Kakami"? ("Thirty Canadians Under Thirty to Watch!" *Maclean's*, January 9, 2006—he'd snuck in under the wire.) And his biggest challenge now was not to let on that he was just going through the motions but to proceed as if it all still did matter.

Look at those kids. The various PAs and gang grips milled around the craft service table—sodden, chilled, full of themselves and non-medicated bison jerky, mentally jerking off to dreams of making a film-fest splash at Sundance, Slamdance, or even Slamdunk, or hanging around the Croissette, aging French movie actresses clutching them briefly to their Dior-scented cheeks while Atom Egoyan raised two fingers in salute and the buzz on the trade-show floor grew deafening. That was why they wanted to make movies—or rather, films—not for the pleasure of the audience or because they had known love.

"P.K.!" The Steadicam guy and the stunt double, a disconcertingly pale, double-jointed woman who went by the name The Body, were playing hackeysack with a vigour born of pent-up energy (sexual? drug-induced? feigned? Can such a thing be feigned?) that Patrick himself hadn't felt for weeks, even months. They gestured to him. *Stoked.* Always stoked. He put his hands to the small of his back, exaggeratedly wincing, indicating no-can-do, and tapped his watch face with what he hoped was a purposeful look.

Patrick Kakami, who had just turned thirty-three two months ago, the same age as Jesus Christ was when he died (and Alexander the Great and John Belushi, men of untethered ambition all—*stoked?*), felt old, much older than he had any right to. It was as if his recently replaced mitral valve had kick-started an accelerated aging process; this ticker he called his "pig heart" triggering a sped-up degeneration of living tissue. Cell death racing along like actors in a Mack Sennett picture. It was 2009. And time itself was melting, oozing over the edge of his days like Dali's clocks.

Patrick made a deal with himself, right there, right then, feet planted in mud, rain misting his rimless glasses, his compromised heart in his mouth, as small and sour as a dried apricot, to reclaim some essential part of himself before it was too late, before the bastards (they, *them*) did him in.

After all, Syd Gross, whom he trusted, who was his friend, had allowed those eunuchs at CBC, their "broadcast partner," to talk him into cutting the scene in *Rain Dog* that meant the most to Patrick—the scene he now thinks of in eulogy as the Rosetta Stone of the entire picture. He couldn't even bear to think about the concessions necessitated by the Chinese co-production deal.

All around him, little dramas, micro-movies, were being played out. Gideon-spouting actor David Mathers was engaged in a flirty game of cat's cradle with the thirteen-year-old Victoria girl who played the novitiate, Sister Incarnata. Mathers with his high beams on, the girl's fingers hopelessly tangled, her laughter like a cat choking on cream. Gita Chapelle, rogue actress, was napping high up in Old Gnarly, one dirty bare foot dangling off her protest platform. The Body pumped her legs like pistons, tossing the footbag from one knee to the other as the nun extras gathered around her counting out loud, urging her on with her pointless task.

The light filtering through the canopy of old-growth cedars and Douglas firs made everything look as if it were being shot in stop-motion. As if all these people were puppets or Claymation figures, their movements exaggerated, grotesque.

Patrick's skin tightened against his skull.

And the first AD still standing there, rattling the script in his face as if he hadn't already answered her question.

Months back, before all the real problems with the production began—before the second female lead took to an enormous Douglas fir, nicknamed Old Gnarly, with a megaphone and an endless supply of energy bars and Red Bull to protest against globalization (as far as Syd knew, she was still up there, may she choke on her armpit hairs), before he had to negotiate the crazy deal points for the director of photography, a high-school pal of Kakami's whose head had swelled to the size of the Stay Puft Marshmallow Man in *Ghostbusters* after working on *Lethal Weapon 4* as the clapper loader (just recalling the initial deal letter made Syd clutch at a phantom pain somewhere in the vicinity of his heart), before Syd found out that Kakami had gone AWOL (as in vanished *without a trace, poof!* as if the man had never existed—described this way to Syd by the hysterical location manager as though Kakami had performed a magic trick)—before all this, before they could secure the permit to shoot on the rainforest island, on native land, Syd Gross had had to attend a sweat lodge ceremony.

How bad could it be, he'd thought, it's just a sauna, right? A friend of his who'd taken part in one during an Outward Bound course said it helped him relieve his aggression. "I didn't feel like killing anyone for about a month," he told Syd.

The only access to the island was by private boat after taking the ferry from the mainland to the Sunshine Coast and driving north, taking yet another ferry, and driving some more. Syd had been told to bring light, comfortable clothing, a gift for the elders (cloth, tobacco), and "no big-city attitude." This was conveyed to him by a spokesman for the Sliammon People, a guy called Porgie, the same man who arrived to pick up Syd and his assistant at the dock on the reserve. ("Have your people call my People," Porgie said afterwards, laughing at his own joke and flashing his teeth.)

Kakami was already on the island, ebullient as usual despite his media rep for a studied cool. He waved around something that looked like a gargantuan cigar. "Grossman!" He jogged towards Syd, his location manager, Drew, drifting along behind him. Drew was a thin, bald Eurasian with hypothyroid Bette Davis eyes who disturbed Syd because he couldn't tell if this Drew person was male or female and was embarrassed to ask anyone, even Patrick.

"These beautiful people, Syd, they've already put us to work. Smell this!" Kakami thrust the oversized cigar thing under Syd's nose. "I made it myself."

He stood there grinning, like a little kid awaiting praise for a kindergarten project.

"It's a smudge stick," Drew told him. "You light it et voila."

"I *know* what it is," said Syd, who had no idea. Was he supposed to smoke it or use it to ream out Kakami for dragging him out to this repository of excessive greenery and spiritual wankery. You want to make a movie about nuns, what's wrong with Montreal or Boston?

He slapped his hands together to change the subject. "So, let's get this fucking show on the road."

His assistant, Helene, the latest in a series of dun-coloured and quietly efficient young women Syd had hired because he found them reassuring, like a school secretary or a crossing guard, pulled him aside. "There's something you need to know about the site of the sweat lodge. These people? They consider it sacred?"

"You're asking me or telling me?"

"I'm just saying, maybe, you know, cut down on the *language* and whatnot?"

Porgie led a small group over to Syd. "Our elder, Charlie Louie," he said, introducing an old man in a blue plaid shirt and saggy jeans, who had the purest white hair Syd had ever seen. The elder held out his hands, palms up. Syd remembered then that he'd forgotten the gift, what was it? Candles? Canned goods? Helene unwound the scarf from around her neck and dangled it in front of him. Hermès—her family must have money. *Note to self*, Syd thought with a flush of bonhomie towards Helene, *possible investors*. He draped the scarf across the elder's palms. "We come in peace," Syd said, and beside him he could feel Helene wincing. The old man smiled and tied the scarf around his head babushka-style, eliciting a round of congenial laughter. There was something about rituals in general that gave Syd the heebie-jeebies, and right now he was feeling them down to his pinky toes.

Porgie introduced the others: a woman with sad eyes whom Syd thought would be attractive enough if she did something with her hair and ditched the shapeless button blanket; a young, broad-shouldered man, hair long and glossy, in a tight T-shirt that read *There Is No Planet B*; another old man, though not as old as Charlie Louie, who was frighteningly obese. Porgie, with his big smile and his annoying habit of lightly touching others on the arm with feigned intimacy, had something of the motivational speaker Tony Robbins about him. Even his teeth looked optimistic, preternaturally white and large. Southern California teeth. Syd had seen enough sets of these to know.

"Nice offering," Kakami said.

"What did you bring?"

"A slide box of Cohíba Esplendidos." Kakami pronounced this in commanding Spanish, practically horking on the *h*. When had he had time to teach himself that?

As Porgie explained the sweat lodge—how it was made with bent willow branches draped with animal hides; the sacred rock pile outside heated by the elder and then carried inside and placed in a hole dug in the centre—Syd felt as if he were back in grade five Social Studies class. The thing actually looked like a grade five Socials project, a dome shape messily covered with skins and army blankets. Kakami, across from him, looked fascinated, though.

"You will experience a purification," Charlie Louie told them. "Some of you maybe even what we call a rebirth—through earth, fire, water, and air. You will get very hot. Just breathe evenly, drink lots of water, pay attention to the elements. If you get too hot, 'Don't Panic,' to quote Douglas Adams. Please feel free to leave." With that, he made his way into the lodge, bending slightly to get through the opening as Porgie held up the flap.

Syd signalled for Helene to go in ahead of him, to case the joint as it were. He was feeling queasy with anxiety. Helene just stood where she was, clutching her day planner to her chest.

"I can't go in. I'm on my moon," she told him.

"You're on what?"

"Her cycle," Kakami said.

"What?"

"She's on the rag," Drew said loudly.

Syd did not want to be listening to this. "How the hell would they know that?"

"They emailed a form and I figured full disclosure was in the spirit of the thing," Helene said. "Don't worry, I filled out yours, too," she added, although this was exactly the kind of thing Syd worried about.

He practically had to crawl into the sweat lodge on his hands and knees, moving from a filtered daylight to deep shade. When the opening flap was lowered, there descended a darkness so intense Syd felt as if he'd dropped ten floors in an elevator. As Charlie Louie muttered what sounded like an incantation or a nursery rhyme, water hit the rocks with a shocking hiss, and the dry, musty, animal-smelling heat became choking wet and tarry.

More steam, and strong smells—body odours and something else, something fecund rising from the earth. Syd was riding a boat along a tributary of the Congo, naked young men poised on the banks with poison arrows. A place Syd had never been, possibly the last place on earth he'd want to go. He even heard the cry of a shrike. He'd had his share of psychotropic experiences, courtesy of his cousin Diggory who'd been the go-to guy in their high-school yeshiva program and was now involved in helpful cosmetic pharmacology, but Syd had never been this inside and outside of himself at the same time.

It felt as if hours had passed, but by his glowing watch dial Syd could see it had been less than fifteen minutes. The sweat in his ear canals trickled, a sensation like blood pooling. Within the scrim of darkness he began to make out forms around him in the lodge, hazy at first and then cohering into solid shapes. He would wonder afterwards if he had been hallucinating, but at the time it all looked so very real. Much later in his life, long after it became clear to him that the things he had witnessed on the island were a kind of twisted gift, he would never completely shake the feeling that somehow the spirits had mistaken him for someone else. Someone more worthy.

He saw a startlingly violet bruise on Drew's previously

flawless neck and a pallor that betrayed low white blood cell counts, her (or his?) already bulging eyes protruded, yellowed in their sockets. Porgie, in a smart suit, was busy thumbing on a BlackBerry, somewhere in bright sunshine. The fat elder's pant leg was pinned up at the left knee, empty. The young muscular guy sat slumped in a jail cell, glossy hair shaved to his scalp, a scar running from lip to right eye, a railroad of track marks on his inner arms. The almost beautiful sad-eyed woman gave off a glow, she was so hugely pregnant.

But when Syd looked towards Kakami he saw nothing. Only heard him, a loud, disembodied voice, talking nonsense: *The darkness represents human ignorance. The sacred site is just one stop along your hero quest towards an authentic life.* Why didn't Porgie or the elder tell him to shut up? Could it be that only he could hear him?

Syd staggered out of the sweat lodge, Kakami's eerie voice in his head, every sense stinging against the open air, and walked shakily through scrub, across the barnacle-encrusted rocks to the shoreline, bivalves breathing so loudly he could hear them—sucking in air, blowing it out. Everything breathing too loudly; his own lungs like bellows stoking a blacksmith's fire. Westward, in the distance, a bald eagle rose, a fat, dripping chum salmon in its grip. Just beyond that, Syd saw a scaly creature lurch from the water, mythic, voracious, a Trump Tower of serrated teeth and shipwrecked breath. It rushed towards the shore, the ocean in its wake rising in a terrifying sheet. Seabirds squawked and wheeled overhead.

The sad-eyed woman—Syd's vision of her, as she was in reality still back in the sweat lodge—now stood on a rocky outcropping, hand on her weighted belly; she opened her mouth, but out came not a scream, nothing so operatic, but a tiny person, curled like a fern. She sent it floating towards Syd on a breeze, buoyant and breathing. Syd turned and ran inland as fast as he could, slack muscles clenching, his breath a living thing, an animal spirit scrabbling for purchase, scraping at his throat.

The others remained in the lodge, sweating, tranquil, and unaware of Syd's terror.

"Sacred sites are traditionally inaccessible to the ignorant and insincere, to the cynical and mean-spirited," Porgie said, flashing those teeth, as he motored them all back across to the reserve's dock a few hours later, after the seafood feast and traditional dancing.

Syd was insincere and cynical, and sometimes even mean-spirited (ignorant, he couldn't credit), so then why him? He wasn't an "honest pilgrim." He was an opportunist, and a good one at that.

All through the celebration he hadn't been able to stop thinking about Drew, the fat man, and the young *Planet B* stud in their dissipation—although Porgie in the bespoke suit and the glowing, sad-eyed woman who had kept looking at him had been disturbing in their own way. Was it some manifestation of the future he'd seen, Syd wondered, not for the last time, or was he just fucked up?

Kakami declared he felt cleansed, while Drew attested to a new sense of calm and opened pores. "I don't think my skin's ever looked so good!" Porgie just smiled that smile of his, and Helene fussed with her day planner.

Syd couldn't head back to Toronto fast enough. He'd gone straight from Pearson International to his box seat at the SkyDome, and afterwards a booth at the Risky Brisket surrounded by women who may or may not have been on their moons, or even on *the* moon, but at least he didn't have to hear about it. *Sacred sites, indeed,* he'd thought, as he raised a glass of his favourite fat, chewy Grenache and toasted civilization.

And now he has to head back into the mouth of the beast. Fucking Kakami.

The story that was bothering Patrick, the one he couldn't shake, he'd overheard on the way over to the Sunshine Coast on the ferry from Horseshoe Bay.

At first he'd thought the two jittery guys mainlining coffee and White Spot fries were film students brainstorming on a title for their yet-to-be-written first feature. They batted names back and forth like a shuttlecock. *Chronic, Genie of the Lamp, White Smurf, Black Bart, Big Buddha Cheese.* When they got to *Oracle Bud,* Patrick finally realized what they were talking about.

"Finest B.C. Kush—beautiful bag appeal, really resinous— all hauled away in garbage bags," one of them had said in an aggrieved tone. It turned out that the "doofus" who tended to the grow-op had fallen asleep reading to his son. ("Remember *Goodnight Moon,* I loved that one. The bowl of porridge and all that shit." "Bowl of mush." "I thought it was porridge." "That was *The Three Bears.*" "I hated that story." "Goodnight Moon would be an awesome name for a band.")

Evidently, the toddler, with the man he knew as Daddo (a.k.a. Frankie) slumbering beside him, had played around with the man's cellphone and managed to speed-dial 911. The police arrived to find no emergency, but rather a distinctive and familiar scent emanating from the basement. One of the guys on the ferry said, "Neighbours told the cops they'd always thought something around the house smelled skunky, but they thought it was a *skunk.*" The other guy snorted. "Skunky!"

What if this Daddo, this Frankie, was the best father in

the world, Patrick had thought, bad career choice notwithstanding?

And where was the mother? How could she not know?

Patrick, who had, up until that moment, been a believer in the church of coincidence, wondered, *what cosmic jester caused things like this to happen?*

Just then, the ferry captain had announced a pod of orcas portside, and the two guys jumped up, sloshing their coffee, newly animated.

"'Baby Beluga,' remember that one? Ralphie somebody."

"Raffi ..."

"That's a guy's name?"

Patrick told all this to the set-dec PA who scrambled along beside him as he strode through dripping fir trees away from the set where the nun extras were gathering for Gong Li's big monologue as the outgoing Mother Superior who has fallen in love with a B.C. permaculturalist. The part about God opening a door when he closes a window.

Or was it the other way around?

"Big Buddha Cheese?" the kid asked.

"Big Buddha Cheese," Patrick said. "But that's beside the point. The point is, will that child, when grown up, ever think: That was the first day of the rest of my life? Think about that."

Patrick was by then loping along so quickly the kid couldn't keep up.

"Where are you going?"

"You tell Sydney Gross," he called back to the PA, "that this is the first day of the rest of my life. And maybe his."

Because.

"Does this mean we're breaking early for lunch?" the kid yelled. But Patrick was gone, swallowed by the trees that remained silent and dripping.

Syd hustles along Hastings, looking to signal a cab. He managed to disentangle himself from the weeping filmmaker after pocketing the man's business card in triplicate ("Reel Pictures." *Real original*, thinks Syd) and making a number of promises he's already consigned to his cranial delete file.

No cabs in sight, and up ahead a mob appears to be moving towards him—placards, banners, cow bells, megaphones, people on stilts dressed as the Grim Reaper and Maggie Thatcher (!?), women juggling fire. Everywhere in this city there always seems to be someone walking on stilts or playing with fire, or both. Jesus Christ, he should've known better. He's walked right into the Occupation.

Evidently an army of career activists along with a number of the genuinely dispossessed took over the streets around the city's historic Woodward's Building in 2002. And here they still are, seven years later. It's become a holy site for some, like Benares. Pilgrims come, drawn by ethical tourism and the revolving red W up on high, and are allowed to pitch their tents after making a donation. The country's poorest postal code now has its own official designation, sort of like the Vatican, a sovereign city state.

The squatters are sponsored by Roots and equipped with the latest in leather backpacks and Che caps. The Dalai Lama has visited, as well as Richard Branson, who arrived in a Virgin hot-air balloon. Buffy Sainte-Marie even tried to adopt half-native triplets whose mother had OD'd shortly after giving birth, but the children were deemed better off being raised in their own culture. It takes a village and all that jazz. Kakami told him this over beers in some atrocious hole with terry-cloth slipcovers over the tables that the director lauded for its authenticity. Patrick was excited about the movie possibilities, but negotiating with the actual squatters was brutal. Their people had *people*. Syd's convinced he could more easily bring the Taliban to heel.

He turns up Cambie to avoid the festivities but there's a broken sewer main flooding the street, carrying with it the effluvia of the Downtown Eastside, a flotilla of cigarette butts, bottles, broken high-heeled shoes, syringes, falafel wrappers, a swollen paperback copy of *The Kite Runner*, and an aluminum crutch. Does he head upriver or turn back and make his way through the crush of demonstrators?

Syd takes one more look at the chanting throng and bends down to roll his sport slacks above his knees. Then, briefcase held high over his head, he begins the portage.

Because.

Because the kernels from the bottom of the popcorn bag at the Ridge had always wedged between his front teeth in a way that felt so good but verged on pain, a pain that he had borne, Patrick thought, rather bravely.

Because of his mother's unexpectedly cool fingers on his lips while they watched late-night movies on the basement television in those weeks leading up to his first surgery, telling him she'd always wanted to be a nun—*but don't tell your father*. How seriously he'd held that secret to his sickly boy chest, *their secret*, as if it had really mattered. Had it even been true? The existence of a cosmic jester never entering his mind back then.

With his pig heart beating time, Patrick Kakami lopes through the island forest that expands around him, sloughing off old skin as if he's a snake.

"The things we do to keep on keepin' on," the helicopter pilot says to Syd over the juddering of the rotors and engine roar. "Me, I pretend I'm choppering over Nam."

"Nam?"

"Viet. Like in that Kakami movie." He makes big googly eyes and waggles his tongue to simulate craziness—at least Syd hopes it's a simulation.

"You mean Coppola." Yet the notion of Kakami making a war movie isn't that far-fetched. He has the earnestness and passion, the requisite sense of moral absolutes that Syd himself lacks. He tightens his seat belt. The blue-green Pacific and rocky island shorelines pierced with towering evergreens are far below. Toy scenery, an art director's mock-ups. There are no more mysteries, the whole wide world is charted and toe-tagged, but that knowledge does little to lessen Syd's unease.

"Ride of the Valkyries" crackles into Syd's headset.

"Don't you love the smell of napalm in the morning!" whoops the pilot, pulling back hard on the joystick.

When Syd had arrived at the Horseshoe Bay ferry terminal by cab a couple of hours earlier, his shoes and socks reeking of sewage, it was mired in chaos. The *Queen of Coquitlam* had rammed the marina, sinking several pleasure craft and damaging the ferry dock. Sailings were cancelled for at least the remainder of the day. People swarmed the wharf, cellphones pressed to temples or thumbs busily texting their loved ones or their lawyers, while gulls wheeled and screeched overhead. Syd bought himself a pair of drugstore sandals and chartered a helicopter to get to the island location.

While he'd waited by the makeshift landing pad beside the ferry terminal's parking lot, two ferret-faced guys sprawled on the curb behind him, slurping coffee and muttering together. One of them shredded a paper napkin as if wreaking vengeance on a life-long enemy. "And that guy who plays Voldemort and calls himself Rafe, what's that about? It's spelled *Ralph*."

His buddy shrugged.

"It's British," Syd said.

"Huh?"

"Ralph Nathaniel Twisleton-Wykeham-Fiennes, eighth cousin to Prince Charles. If you go in for that kind of thing."

"Twinkletoes? Effin' Brits. That is just so *wrong*."

The other guy eyed Syd suspiciously. "How do you know that?"

"I'm a movie producer."

They had looked him over: his orange-and-green flip-flops and rolled-up, sewage-splotched pants, his shirt half hanging out over the front of the slacks—and guffawed. "Yeah right." One of them had proffered him a fat joint.

In the confines of the helicopter, the cheap sandals exude a warm rubber smell that clogs Syd's nostrils. And they're giving his toes wedgies. He's so uncomfortable he may as well add a butt thong and call it a day. Syd feels naked, almost impotent, stuck in a shuddering tin can half a mile above sea level with a madman, his feet exposed—their pale flesh and untended toenails proclaiming: Here is a man no longer in complete control of the situation. If only he'd stayed wharf-side in his own stinking hand-stitched Italian footwear with Cheech and Chong Jr., fired up the doobie (*did people still call them doobies?*), and said to hell with Kakami, the production, and the whole freaking business.

"Island looks bigger," Syd says on approach, the helicopter still in one piece despite the pilot's Kilgore impressions.

"Always does from the air."

"I thought it was supposed to be the other way around."

As they circle lower, Syd sees something far below in a clearing moving swiftly. A deer, a bobcat?

"Someone's in an awful hurry," says the pilot.

A man?

"Mr. Gross? Mr. Gross!" The first AD, with her truncheon-wielding Afrikaner accent, moves in on Syd as he lurches from the helicopter. She runs hunched over, one hand holding down her frothing mass of hair, the other waving a clipboard, pages fluttering from it crazily in the downdraft. Drew follows, sobbing, and a pissed-off David Mathers, complaining in a loud, over-enunciating voice that he's due to shoot a guest spot for *Little Mosque on the Prairie* in two weeks less a day and this better not yada, contract, yada yada, residuals, et cetera. A pale, double-jointed woman in a glittering gymnastics leotard appears at Syd's elbow, whispering (*why whispering?*) something about a Cirque de Soleil audition, a once-in-a-lifetime opportunity. The nuns, all in swimsuits or yoga gear, swarm over. The Stay Puft–headed DOP brings up the rear, piggybacking a teenaged girl, the Victoria jailbait who plays the baby nun.

They converge on Syd like a kind of ooze, their hopes and dreams, their messy lives, their *schedules* thrust at him as if he were Jesus Christ Superstar healing lepers. Syd holds out his hands, palms outward, both steadying himself and fending them off. The helicopter tilts up and away behind him.

One by one the actresses who play the nuns turn blue-grey and waterlogged. They flop onto their backs or fronts, still and swollen, seemingly floating. The first AD opens her mouth, tongue clawing for air. Out of her left nostril scuttles a small brown crab, followed by another and another. The DOP has a gash in his gut where it's been impaled by a tree branch. It sticks out the other side, looking for all the world like a cheap illusionist's trick, save for the all-too-real blood. Minutes pass, or hours, then, as if someone's pulled focus and upped the volume, they're all their own clamouring selves again.

The weather is unseasonably warm for early October; the air on Syd's toes disconcerting but not entirely unpleasant. "Okay,

okay. Can someone tell me exactly what's going on?" Please God, no, not the squawk. He sounds like a seagull. "When was the last time anyone saw Kakami?"

The ghostly gymnast places a hand on Drew's chest. "Breathe. In through the nose, out through the mouth." Syd resists the urge to give the distressed location manager a hug. He's through with dispensing hugs.

"One minute he was standing right there." After another intake and outtake of air, Drew points towards a spot a few feet away. "And the next minute—"

"I know, *poof*, gone, without a trace. Not even a whiff of sulphur."

Drew crosses his (her?) arms. "You don't have to believe me. I know what I saw."

The first AD is composed but seething; her hair appears to move of its own accord, like a nest of vipers. "I was conferring with Mr. Kakami about the shooting script late-morning but he appeared distracted. He cut the scene in which Mother Superior has the vision of playing soccer with the Shaolin monks. Without any explanation. Miss Gong Li refuses to come out of her yurt."

"Let me think," Syd says. "All of you, go. Frolic, yoga, or whatever it is you do for fun here. Just let me think a minute."

A kid, some PA or other in a *Rain Dog* T-shirt, orange hair shaved to his scalp, round blue eyes like a baby's, shyly approaches him. "Mr. K. talked to me right before he disappeared. He told me only to tell you. The stuff he told me."

"So, tell me."

The boy moves closer, taking up a greater portion of Syd's personal space than he deems kosher. Syd inches back gingerly, like you would from an unpredictable small animal clutching a treasure to its chest, maybe a squirrel with a nut. "He talked about everything. He talked about love. He made me see things aren't always the way they seemed." The boy is flushed, his tone reverent, speaking with a kind of dangerous devotion that makes Syd wonder what had been going on on this island these past few weeks. "His voice, it was like he was all voice, you know. I'd never noticed that about him before."

"He talked to you about love?"

"It's not what you think. It was pretty general, not advice about girls and stuff. I know that doesn't make sense, but I can't explain it the way he did. And he told me to tell you, 'This is the first day of the rest of my life.' And maybe yours."

"Yours?"

"No, *yours*."

So no magical disappearing act after all—sudden, but not entirely uncalculated.

Above them, high in Old Gnarly, Gita Chapelle stirs on her platform and calls down through her megaphone, "It's karma, man!" She sounds as if she's woken up from a year-long nap.

"Someone, you"—Syd points to a teamster who's leaning against a tree working his way through a book of Sudoku puzzles—"get me a ladder."

"Union regulations—"

"Stick your union up your ass!" In Syd's rage the squawk is transformed into something terrifying, even grand—the ugly duckling now a beautiful but pissed-off swan.

The PA materializes in front of Syd with an extension ladder under his arm. In the muted, rainforest light he looks like a younger Kakami. The teamster mutters, "Scab," and goes back to chewing on his pencil.

"What's your name? I want to remember it when we're cutting cheques."

"Ivan. Ivan O'Neil. You're going to find him?"

"I'm going to find him and then I'm going to wring his fucking neck."

There is no time for Syd to process that he's climbing a tree in bare feet in the middle of nowhere as he struggles onto Gita Chapelle's platform and grabs her megaphone. "Kakami! Patrick Kakami!!"

Silence, save for the distant surf and the occasional forced screech from the scattering nuns as the DOP runs about goosing them, a rabid fox in the henhouse.

"KA-KAAA-MIIIII!"

Somewhere, far from shore, a glistening chinook salmon twists in a neat double helix through the water. Singing about oceans. Singing about love.

Because.

Because here is the movie, all around us. Here is the neverending story. Patrick shoots and edits simultaneously as he moves through the rainforest, effortlessly synching sound with picture. Here there are no cuts, no retakes, no stopping to powder the immobile brows of Botoxed beauties, to reload film, to change a light gel, to wait around all afternoon for an all-too-brief magic hour in order to score the money shot.

The layers of sound this deep in the forest are phenomenal. Even the mushrooms sing their song, in dozens of fungal dialects all eager to be heard. The lichen and the tree moss, hanging like Triton's beard, fizz and whisper. Here filtered light colludes with leaf and fern, evoking a sensation akin to being in the womb. Here is the green force that drives a fuse through every flower—both redeemer and destroyer.

Patrick begins a tracking shot of this city of trees to rival the fetishized one in *I Am Cuba*.

This one's for dreaming sons and their mothers everywhere—
And where he stops, nobody knows.

"You'll want some real shoes." Porgie rummages around in his rowboat, the inside of which is a midden of thrift-store castoffs and ropes of varying thickness. He hands Syd a well-worn pair of some kind of high-tech hiking boot. They're surprisingly comfortable, considering he isn't wearing socks and the tongues and laces are stiff and crusty with dried seawater.

After an hour or so of placating cast and crew, enduring the amplified taunts of Gita Chapelle and the biblically infused curses of David Mathers, and trying to reach an uncharacteristically AWOL Helene in Toronto, Syd had called the only person in the vicinity he could trust, and who also had a BlackBerry. His relief on seeing the Sliammon man with his whitening-strip smile and his sardonic brown eyes putter into sight from across the water was embarrassing—like a small child finally spying his misplaced mother across the crowded expanse of a shopping mall and wetting himself, having spent long fretful minutes clutching at women wearing the same familiar sky-blue stretch pants but with shocking, non-mother faces.

Porgie didn't let on that there was anything out of the ordinary happening. Or maybe he thought this crisis was par for the course on film shoots. "So you need a guide?" he'd asked. "A real, live, honest Injun?"

They started out in the direction Ivan O'Neil said Kakami was headed, although Syd thought the running man he'd seen from the helicopter had been going the opposite way. The PA wanted to go with them, but Porgie needed someone to watch his outboard motor. "Anyone touches that Johnson has some seriously bad Coast Salish mojo coming down on them. You tell them that." Syd feels for the kid, ever consigned to being the messenger. And he probably quit a job as a bike courier to take this gig.

As they move farther into the rainforest, Syd can't shake the feeling he's travelling upriver, even though there is no river and there is no actual up or down either, as far as he can tell. Porgie holds aside low-lying branches that lash back at Syd if he doesn't move quickly enough. After an hour or so, the island larger even than it had looked from the air, Porgie says, "The last time I went this far across the island was when I was thirteen and we were searching for my auntie. The same thing happened then. The island kept growing around us, helping hide her."

So it's not Syd's fatigue and rage and disorientation—the forest is alive, or rather, more perversely alive than it has any right be. That he so readily accepts this as a fact is something he'll spend a lot of time thinking about later in life. "What happened?"

"She didn't want to be found."

Porgie eventually announces they have to bed down for the night, the darkness is that complete. Syd, who hasn't slept outdoors since a mismanaged bar mitzvah camp-out in the ravine behind his grandparents' Rosedale house when he was thirteen—one that involved improperly disposed of smoked-meat remains, a couple of raccoons, and a small family pet with the unfortunate name of Brisket—hears all manner of amplified and unidentifiable sounds in the surrounding night. Flesh-eating plants busily masticating the remains of rodents; antean beasts lying in wait; the long-lost auntie, now spectral and gone feral, watching, as if watching could be called a sound. *Here be monsters.* Porgie refused to light a fire, saying it would disturb the balance in the forest.

Syd forces himself to focus on his guide's cheerful

disembodied voice. "My grandfather Charlie's not too happy about it but I feel like I've put in my time on the reserve. Also, I can bring some new perspective to the biz, right?" Syd drifts off to Porgie confessing his dream: to be a producer/director of broad Hollywood comedies, a First Nations Ivan Reitman (Porgie's own analogy).

Syd will have to talk him out of it. Look at me, he'll say, it's not all power lunches at Orso and hot-buttered premieres. It's whiny people wanting a pound of flesh every day. It's the studios in the States, and the broadcasters and government funding agencies here squeezing your nuts. It's the Chinese co-producers politely insisting you use the crap-ass stock from FortuneFilm—a subsidiary of DoubleHappinessCo—which Syd suspects is made by blind orphans in a Shenzhen factory that also manufactures Barbie accessories brightened with lead-based paints.

It's this: the most talented filmmaker you've ever worked with, a man you consider a friend, maybe your best friend, dropping a few gnomic utterances and making for the bush.

Don't get Syd wrong. He adores the idea of movies, loves the act of watching them. But movie people? Janus-faced actors and the high-level technicians with their intense Asperger's-like shoptalk jack up his acid reflux. The unions suck the magic out of moviemaking—teamsters can't pass gas without consulting their local; IATSE members become apoplectic if someone other than an IATSE Nazi dares touch a light switch. It's all more Jimmy Hoffa than Norma Rae.

Screenwriters act all docile but would stick a fork between your eyes if they could get away with it. Directors and DOPs with their childlike ids and grandiose sense of entitlement remind Syd of the destructive, drooling baby in that early Pixar short, the one that terrorized the poor tin soldier. Writer-directors—*auteurs*—don't even get him started.

Patrick Kakami had been different—*is* different. Why is he thinking about him in the past tense? Surely he isn't dead? What was it Kakami had said in the sweat lodge? Maybe he should've listened? Syd can still hear the voice but not the words as he floats along in his sleep.

Naked young men holding poison blow darts line the dark river, waiting for Syd to make a wrong move, while Porgie continues to parse the overlooked *mise en scène* of *Kindergarten Cop* long into the porous night.

Syd's watch has stopped and his BlackBerry's not working. According to Porgie, who purports to have some facility with reading the sun, they've been trailing Kakami for about forty-two hours. Which isn't possible as the island is only twelve kilometres total in circumference, give or take, and so narrow they should be able to hear the tide moving in and out, the cannibal shrieks of gulls. In a movie this would be the point where one of them spots remnants of their old campfire and loudly exclaims that they've been travelling in circles, upon which the two wanderers commence squabbling about what an idiot the other guy is and smack each other around and either make up or storm off in opposite directions only to meet up again later to dispatch a common enemy. But there are, of course, no campfire remains here, no *here* here, and all the trees look the goddamn same to Syd, so they may or may not have been going in circles. His bowels are so tight; he's eaten enough salmon jerky to embalm his colon. The loud silence of the rainforest, when Porgie isn't talking, triggers his tinnitus, so that there's a one-man klezmer band going on inside his head.

Porgie stops and drops his pack to the ground by an enormous fallen tree bristling with mushrooms growing sideways from the trunk like petrified mouths. The yellowed fungi smirk at Syd, issuing a kind of dare.

"The rest of the journey you'll have to make on your own," Porgie says. "There's the site of an ancient village somewhere west of here, and a warning about not disturbing the souls of the dead. It's just a story the toothless ones tell. I'm not a superstitious guy, but I grew up with this stuff and it's hard to shake. Plus I promised Grandfather Charlie." He flashes a hardcover of Jerry Weintraub's *When I Stop Talking, You'll Know I'm Dead.* "I'll wait for you here. Catch up on my reading."

Syd really should just punch Porgie. *Clock him.* Force him to lead the way at gunpoint. He aims for levity instead. "If I don't come back, my people will be calling your People." *Funny guy, that Syd.* Maybe, just maybe, someone will remember to say that at his memorial service.

"Bear hug." When Porgie holds out his arms, Syd doesn't resist. Porgie sends him on his way with a water canteen, more salmon jerky, a flashlight, a foil astronaut blanket, and some advice: "Follow the money." Those teeth. Must be some sweet dental plan on the reserve.

The rainforest thickens, grows primeval as Syd traverses it solo, the vegetation ever larger and more lurid, as if he's working his way back to the beginnings of time. The sun can no longer penetrate, even though he knows it's there above the twisted forest canopy. This is the darkness and dank not of night, but of a daytime basement, with the nearest source of light far away at the top of the stairs. The flashlight is small and doesn't cut much of a swath; Syd soon gives up on it, shoving it into a pocket. There are shapes and shadows, much like when he was in the sweat lodge, and they eventually coalesce into more solid forms. Snakes, and something that swoops by on wings—bird or bat?

A larger creature takes shape in the near distance, like a daydream nightmare, something resembling a tapir with its saggy snout, but also sporting boar-like tusks and scales. The armoured beast moves purposefully towards him, though Syd can't exactly call it *charging* as it's moving in slow motion, and he thinks, for a moment, that it's merely a test drive of some proto-4D CGI that will pass harmlessly through him while he continues on his way. The Early Pleistocene creature is soon upon him, its breath carting the reek of the Augean stables. Syd feels for the flashlight. A light in the animal's eyes might divert it, send it squealing and crashing into the trees. But Syd, as he knows all too well, has simply watched too many movies.

There's an explosion (Syd's brain imploding? The life force propelled from his body like so much jetsam? The world itself ending not with a whimper but a bang?) and the tapir-creature lies at his feet, scaly sides heaving. A person in camo pants, a flak vest, and a pith helmet better suited to the long bar at Raffles Hotel circa 1912 jumps upon it and works a knife into its throat.

She—for it is a she, with blond pigtails spronging from under her headgear and a small, tidy frame; the kind of woman who'd ordinarily be deemed girlish, although there's nothing girlish about the hunter—wipes the bloodied knife across her knee and addresses Syd, who's curled up on the ground in the requisite fetal position, curled so compactly he feels almost yogic. "You are on a vision quest?"

"No." Syd sits up, attempting that in-through-the-nose-out-through-the-mouth breathing thing to quell the onset of arrhythmia, as his blood pounds in loop-de-loops through his arterial walls.

The tapir-creature looks smaller than it had in life, nothing more than an armadillo with a homelier face. Is this what Syd was terrified of? Just behind the hunter there's a rifle propped against a dead doe, the animal's legs bound together and tied to a long, thick branch. Interestingly, congealed blood smells exactly like Syd always imagined it would: a thick, sharp stink, like hot, pissed-upon copper.

"I'm looking for someone. A colleague. A friend." My antagonist. My albatross. Something in Syd, the incessant rage perhaps, has been displaced, shunted aside, by a kind of poetic sorrow.

"Another white man?" the hunter asks, even though she's white herself. Disconcertingly Scandinavian-looking, almost as pale as the sequinned gymnast back at the *Rain Dog* shoot.

"You saw him? Was he all right?"

"He didn't look robust, if that's what you're asking, but men of the spirit seldom are. How that man could talk, though!"

"Did he talk to you about love?"

"Love? Nothing so base and fleeting. Your friend has a larger sense of purpose. To love is too binding, too temporal. To seek is what makes us uniquely human. An animal may love, but can it seek?"

Syd seeks. Does this make him special, too, somehow enlightened? What he is, is enlightened to the unavoidable fact that the doe is rotting. Syd wonders how long the hunter has been heaving it around the endless forest. From her way of talking, he's guessing about a hundred years.

As she continues her prolix speech, Syd sees her not as she is, but cleaned up, in a white bed, in a room with institutional green walls, her head bound with gauze, her wild eyes no longer roaming their sockets. She drones on about Kakami's conviction and beliefs, and it takes some force of will for Syd to not drift off as tired as he is and as potently soporific as the strange hunter is turning out to be. The thing to do would be to bury the sorry little armadillo with its anteater snout and be on his way.

"Which way did he go?"

"Directions? What are directions, really? Human constructs! He simply left when the time came to depart."

"And when was this?"

"A fortnight ago, I believe." She sits examining her gun, perched on the deer's liquefying carcass, the insects of the rainforest threading their way through the body, an army bent on fortification, nothing more.

A fortnight? What the hell was that? Four days? A week? The memory of a recent award-winning HBO mini-series, adapted from a forgotten Victorian novel, something involving a highwayman and a woman with royal complications in her blood, works its way towards him, like a man crawling on his belly across the desert.

A *fortnight* as in two bloody weeks?

The next morning, or the one after that, as the trees thin out before him, there is the shoreline in the distance, the edge of the island, a geographic entity Syd has despaired of seeing again. He considers dropping to his hands and knees Pope-like and kissing the ground.

But it's too soon to rejoice. Rising against the lighted shore is a monstrous apparition. A glistening black figure, dripping with seaweed, misshapen, with a hunched back and a single tusk protruding from its deformed head. The warrior spirit that stalks the island, meting out justice to those who trespass on the sacred burial grounds. It strides slowly up the beach in Syd's direction, and his heart, which until now has pretty damn gamely withstood the various shocks and indignities of this island, begins to bleat weakly, like a lost lamb.

The creature stops and appears to be removing its own head, complete with the tusk!

And Syd is thinking not *now the picture will never be finished,* or *I'll never see Kakami again,* but that he will never *hear* him. Because the kid was right: Kakami is a voice— ebullient, believing, his vision persuasive. It has led Sydney Gross this far, to an ending befitting the hero of a quest. A death in Technicolor, by the sea, by the hand of a mythical creature.

He shades his eyes. A woman stands on the beach, scuba mask in hand, shrugging off the straps of her oxygen tank and lowering the apparatus to the ground. She peels off her wetsuit. Even from this distance Syd can tell she's gorgeous, and almost instantly his fear is transformed into an incredible horniness, his cock pressing anxiously against his stiff and journey-stained underwear. If he had a choice between her and Kakami he knows exactly who he would choose. If he had a choice.

Divested of her gear, she beckons to someone on a small yacht in the distance and settles herself upon the sand.

Outside the cave where Syd Gross finds Patrick Kakami, there are no heads on stakes, shrunken and blackened by the sun. No preserved lips revealing thin white lines of teeth, smiling in eternal slumber. Not that Syd expected to see anything like that, but still.

The two men sit side by side in the cave, images flickering against the walls from a small fire. "The perfect moving picture," Kakami says.

"Kind of puts both of us out of a job."

They sit some more in silence. Finally, Syd asks, "So you were really pissed at me?"

"About what?"

"That scene we cut. For the CBC presale."

"Oh, *that*." Kakami rolls his eyes. "You know I have this pig heart, right?"

"It's just a bit of tissue."

"A pig died so I could live, Grossman. What do you think about that?"

"I'm not an observant Jew. Pigs have died so I could live. I eat bacon. I eat bacon *with* dairy. Prosciutto wrapped around washed-rind cheeses."

"That's not what I mean. I've been thinking about things. Like, am I now more than one species? Will my child be part pig?"

"What child?"

"Hypothetically, Syd."

"I think about stuff, too."

"Not really."

"Okay, I didn't used to."

"Meaning?"

"Now? I see things."

"Dead people?" Kakami laughs. This acerbic quality is new. Or new-*ish*.

"You could put it that way."

Scenes from Indonesian shadow plays, O. Selznick's burning of Atlanta, the telephone call from Paris, Texas, Walt's hippos in tutus, Lillian Gish in silent anguish, Harry and Sally in a clinch are reflected on the cave walls. A never-ending story.

"A man can change," Kakami says.

Was all this supposed to change him? Was that the point? If this were a movie, Syd would emerge from the cave to marry the glowing Coast Salish woman and become an honorary tribal member, maybe even an elder, the Oracle of Sliammon. Patrick would be best man in absentia. That floating fern could be his child. He would catch it as it drifted through the air like dandelion fluff and hold it gently to his chest. Porgie would go on to produce *FUBAR: Haida Gwaii*, with a cameo by Bill Murray, and bring in the biggest Canadian English-language box office ever.

But Syd likes himself the way he is.

"Do you know what you're doing?" he asks Kakami, almost in a whisper.

"Perfectly."

Far across the Pacific, where the Sliammon and the Haisla and the Mayans and the Mesopotamians and the naysayers of Pythagoras and all the rest of us once thought there was a ledge where things simply surrendered to gravity and tipped off into a void, an endless waterfall carrying with it the detritus of civilizations that ventured too far, there's a tremor the seismograph on nearby Texada Island registers as 8.7 on the Richter scale.

Hours later, water will rise and darken the horizon, rushing towards the flickering point of light in the cave like a berserk colossus on a surfboard. Before this, though, Syd will have spent hours saying all the right things, trying to persuade Kakami to leave the cave. The options for Syd Gross will dwindle down to three: (a) bodily wrestle Kakami out into the light and drag him back across the island, (b) stay here for as long as forever lasts, watching the end credits roll, or (c) go, quickly, and warn the rest about the things he has seen.

DRAMATIS PERSONÆ

The Children of Arcadia Court

Bashaar Khan (14, athlete & dancer)
inhabited by Zachriel (an empathetic angel)

Stephan Choo (12, good student)
inhabited by Elyon (a practical & vengeful angel)

Leo Costello Jr. (14, nice dude)
inhabited by Barman (a learned angel)

Jason Wadsworth a.k.a. The Wad (15, school bully)
inhabited by Yabbashael (a cheerful angel)

Jessica Wadsworth (15, Jason's twin, anorexic)
inhabited by Rachmiel (a merciful angel)

The Others

Gary, Lubbock, and Sweeney a.k.a. The Three Wise Men
(homeless men living in the rough)

Cullen (16, Jessica's boyfriend)

Gabriel (an archangel and head messenger)

Also featuring various parents, grandparents,
and other antagonists

WE COME IN PEACE

Errare humanum est. Perseverare diabolicum.
—ZACHRIEL

Unlike Baal and Asmodeus, we were not, *are* not, fallen angels.
Not even Rachmiel, who no longer resides among us.

It began with an old man, a man who had spent his life
editing moving pictures in early Bollywood, before sound—and
afterwards as well, but with less satisfaction. He could not stop
thinking about the bitter taste of black walnuts on his tongue.
As he worked there had always been a bowl at his elbow, and
he cracked the walnuts in his left fist. This was what he missed
most about being alive. His yearning was a magnetic storm, a
riptide. We were infected with longing as if by a mighty plague.
Then there were the others with their baked beans, their goat
curries, their steel-cut oats with maple syrup, even the recol-
lected taste of their own blood.

Bitter, sweet, salty, sour. Just when we thought we understood, that we could arrest the contagion, it was rumoured

there was a fifth flavour. *Umami*. How was it mortals could conceive of a fifth taste when all of the heavenly host could not?

There we were, in the grip of an intense curiosity about the senses that had been tamped down since time began. Sight and sound we could almost comprehend, but taste and smell, and, most unfathomable of all, touch—how was it these things could conjure ecstasy and revulsion in equal measure? (The Christ, who had suckled at the teat and could have spoken to the matter from experience, is such an ascetic that he remained silent when quizzed about the wine, unleavened bread, and olives, not to mention the fine ointments administered by women's hands. The pain and suffering, on the other hand, these he never minded sharing.)

The five of us—Barman, Elyon, Rachmiel, Yabbashael, and Zachriel—were selected as emissaries. (Note to Gabriel: *conscripts* would have been a more appropriate term. Or *guinea pigs*.)

Lacking corporeality, we have no distinguishing physical characteristics, but, unlike the sentinels and tutelary geniuses, we messengers do have traits that set us apart. In our small group Barman is the preternaturally intelligent one; Elyon, the efficient and vengeful one (best known for bringing the plague of hail upon Egypt); Rachmiel, the merciful one; Yabbashael, the cheerful one; and Zachriel, the understanding one (for comparable empathy, Barman says, one has to look to Commander Troi from the American television series *Star Trek: The Next Generation*).

We have no gender, of course, but on Arcadia Court we became four teenaged boys and a girl. At the time that distinction meant nothing to us. With at least 3.8 million millennia of combined experience, the one thing we had never suspected we were was naive.

The morning we arrived, a number of things happened—or didn't happen—inside the homes on the quiet cul-de-sac of Arcadia Court that the observant might have recognized as miracles.

Bashaar Khan had gone to bed the previous night with a new eruption of acne across his cheeks but woke with clear skin, a fact he celebrated by working an excessive amount of "product" into his dark hair until it resembled the varnished shell of a rhinoceros beetle. Stephan Choo's mother did not have to carry her son's bedding straight to the laundry room, holding it at arm's length to maximize her distance from the sadly familiar acrid smell. Leo Costello Jr. did not begin the day by giving his little sister and brother the usual cheerful noogies, so that their wailing did not wake their parents and the family members ended up clambering into their lease-to-own Ford Escape later than usual. This gave them the opportunity to witness the hitherto mythic shopping-cart racers hurtling down Mountain Highway, daredevil homeless men who had, as Leo Sr. said, "obviously nothing left to lose." They collected bottles and dwelt in the rough of Hastings Creek where the children of Arcadia Court were frequently warned not to go.

And, perhaps most significant, Jessica Wadsworth sat down and ate breakfast for the first time in three years. Her brother, Jason—whom we would shortly learn was almost exclusively referred to as The Wad—greeted his parents not with a grunt but with a beatific smile. This inspired his mother to head to his room to ransack it for illegal drugs and drug paraphernalia, while his father turned to Jason's twin sister, urging Jessica to take another helping of yogurt and muesli.

"Do we have any walnuts, Father?" Jason asked. "Or baked beans, perchance?"

"Oh my God," his mother yelled from the hallway. "It's the

munchies!" There ensued a spirited debate between the two adults about whether crystal methamphetamine caused the munchies or whether that was just pot. (*"Just* pot? Is that like *just* one more before hitting the road?")

That Thursday was, as Barman, our specialist on world religions, later pointed out, the Catholics' Feast of Scholastica, patron saint of convulsive children. "Isn't that ironic?" But when asked in what way, Barman, being new to the concept, just shrugged.

To err is human, to forgive divine. That old trout. We can tell you now that it's the other way around; a complex vice versa.

We hope the records will show that what we did was undertaken not as a lark but in the true spirit of exploration. In other words, like Vasco da Gama and Neil Armstrong, we were *sent.*

That first morning the rain and the smell of damp cedar and the ozone-charged air overwhelmed our just-awakened senses. How can we explain it? It was as if magma flowed in our veins, rather than blood.

And everywhere the taste of the undiscovered was practically vibrating on our tongues.

Our first heady days went by in a blur of rampaging sensations so intense we thought we could understand how overwhelmed autistic children must feel, or someone newly awakened from a coma who finds himself on the streets of Pamplona during the festival of the bulls. But one particular day does stand out: February 14, St. Valentine's Day, 2011.

It was only our third day of school, a Monday. We'd had a relatively quiet weekend after the initial tumult of familiarizing ourselves with the young people whose bodies we now inhabited. Rachmiel and Yabbashael were hosted by the fifteen-year-old twins Jessica and Jason Wadsworth. The former was a small, winter-melon-coloured thing with brittle hair, thinned flesh stretched over pointy bones, veins cross-hatched under the surface of her skin. As if they were siblings in a nursery rhyme or biblical parable, her brother, in contrast, was a ruddy young ox, golden hair razed close to the scalp, a boy whose idea of a joke was to stick a tree-trunk leg out from under a cafeteria table, trip up a student carrying a loaded tray, and gaze around in feigned bewilderment.

Zachriel was now Bashaar Khan, who was handsome in a fourteen-year-old way and knew it. Athletic and talented in the arts, he was a boy destined to make his mark. Some older youths from the North Vancouver musallah had noticed Bashaar's capabilities as well and had launched a stealth campaign to radicalize him. Fully enamoured of Western excess, Bashaar had so far rebuffed their advances.

Barman was inhabiting Leo Costello Jr., a shaggy-haired boy of fourteen who was as agile as he was quick-witted, and loved, or at least tolerated, by everyone, it seemed, save his younger brother and sister. We couldn't help but notice that of all our hosts Barman's was the most congenial. ("A match made in heaven," Barman agreed.)

And Elyon had borrowed the body of Stephan Choo, the only progeny of an aging couple originally from Guangzhou who had given up on having children when unexpectedly blessed with Stephan. An intelligent, much-adored, and coddled boy, he had trouble navigating the shoals of childhood. Although only twelve, Stephan was completing his first year of high school, in the same grade eight class as Leo Jr., due to a well-intentioned school board initiative called "acceleration."

Stephan's only valentine cards that day were from the school librarian and the rest of us. "You got a valentine from The Wad and The Stick Insect?" asked one incredulous backbencher, a boy with a lazy eye and a hairstyle we came to know as a faux-hawk. He plucked from Stephan's hand the cards he had received from the twins, rather modest declarations of friendship from cartoon characters named SpongeBob and Squidward. It was fortunate he didn't notice the ones from Bashaar and Leo Jr., one featuring a prancing pony with the words, "I sure get a KICK out of you! Be My Valentine!" inside the stylized shape of a heart, and the other a sock-puppet mermaid: "You're my FISH come true!"

The heart, we were to learn, is a lonely muscle.

As soon as school let out that afternoon, Stephan was surrounded by a group of boys making off-colour suggestions about various activities he might get up to with the twins. They tied him to the neglected tetherball post in the far end of the sports field with a skipping rope and subjected him to a vigorous round of three-on-three. By the time Leo Jr. and Bashaar intervened, the boys had fled hooting and there was a puddle on the cracked asphalt around Stephan's feet.

It seemed nothing in Herodotus, Sun Tzu, or even Revelation had adequately prepared us for teenaged mores and the indignities of Elysium Heights Secondary.

Adjusting to our bodies at the beginning was difficult. No longer discarnate, we had to focus on negotiating doorways and stairwells. Bruises bloomed on our hips and shins like exotic fungi. Jason had a split lip and a black eye, and was summoned to the principal's office to be quizzed about whom he'd been fighting *this time*. Bashaar, a.k.a. Bash, a power forward on the school's basketball team though only in grade nine, found himself warming the bench. (The militant musallah youths took the opportunity to milk this: "In Mecca, true believers are not *benched* ...") Stephan had a reputation for being clumsy, so no one, not even his parents, thought anything of it when he broke his glasses three times in one week.

And all that effluvia. Sweat, nocturnal emissions, the transit of liquids and solids from one end to the other. The human body, a moody and capricious marvel. It is little wonder St. Francis called his own Brother Ass. (One of Barman's favourite authors, the late American satyr Henry Miller, wrote, "To relieve a full bladder is one of the great human joys." A sentiment worthy of a T-shirt, Yabbashael noted after one particularly satisfying visit to the second-floor boys' room.

The amount of time we spent behind bathroom doors did not go unnoticed. It was the worst for Rachmiel. Years of deprivation had left her host, Jessica's, digestive system as fragile as Malaysia's ravaged mangrove forests, her newly robust appetite triggering bouts of gastrointestinal distress and vomiting. And now that she was no longer anorexic, it wasn't long before she finally began menstruating. This discomfited some of us more than it did Rachmiel.

"The array of feminine hygiene products at the Lynn Valley Centre's Shoppers Drug Mart is staggering," Rachmiel told us, eyes as round and darkly glistening as a mouse lemur's. "An entire aisle."

To which Yabbashael, a.k.a. The Wad, speaking for the rest of us, said: "TMI, dear *sister*, TMI."

How mystifying it is that knowledge and experience are such utterly different beasts—one a contemplative water buffalo, the other a wild mink.

Why Arcadia Court? Why not Jammu, the ancestral home of our black-walnut-loving tempter? Or Barcelona or Manhattan where our taste receptors might have been set abuzz? Why not an outpost in sub-Saharan Africa where we might have been of some use?

The truth is that like a child spinning a globe, eyes closed tight, the compact planet skimming rapidly under his index finger until it slows and then stops (There! The Bonin Islands? Wuhan? Tucuruí? The world suddenly seeming larger than large, wanderlust abruptly sated), our choice of destination was rather whimsical. And we did like the name and the way clouds sat low on the mountaintop just above that enclave in North Vancouver. There was, we admit, a waft of something compelling from a small wooded area nearby, beside Hastings Creek. "The smell of destiny," Rachmiel had called it, rather portentously, considering we could not yet smell anything in the literal sense. At the time, we believed destiny to be one of those weasel words beloved by those with little insight into the workings of the universe.

Our fact-finding mission was to last as long as it took to discover the zenith of each human sense. Barman's best guess was four years; Elyon thought a week or so should do it. At any rate, time had, for us, never been of consequence. Now we were to be human in all respects, bound to the limitations of the species—no being in two places at once, no interventions, no miracles.

Arcadia Court itself comprised just seven houses arrayed around a horseshoe-shaped road opening off Arcadia Drive, which lay between the steeply graded and winding Mountain Highway and Lynn Valley Road. It had a neat little physicality to it, a sense of order challenged by the surrounding wilderness.

It was during our second week there that we first wandered into the forbidden woods by Hastings Creek. Almost hidden amidst the foliage, in a clearing on the east side of the creek, a soiled blue plastic tarp strung between two hemlocks caught our eyes. And from under it came guttural laughter, voices simultaneously muted and oddly amplified. "Here, mix these two together and now try it," said one, followed by a sidewinder of a cough, while someone else gagged.

Yabbashael went first, fording the creek without even bothering to take off Jason's prized Air Jordans. Stumbling over a pile of debris, Yabbashael sent empty bottles and cans clattering in the relative silence of the clearing. Three old men emerged from under the tarp, red faced, two of them with matted greyish-brown beards, all looking as if they were wearing clothing made of sodden cardboard.

"Shit, kid, we're trying to have a board meeting here," said the bald, leather-faced one, waving in Yabbashael's direction a bottle with a cigarette butt (or a fly?) floating in it. A decidedly human pong swirled about the men, a cloud of urine, sweat, and cigarette smoke.

And that is how we met the *genius loci* of Hastings Creek, the near-mythical shopping-cart racers of Lynn Valley. They were the kind of men the Christ would have consorted with, and who could blame him? They were the lepers, the untouchables, of this place, and so forbidden fruit to us.

Yabbashael and Barman were particularly drawn to the Three Wise Men, as they took to calling their new friends. To this day, Yabbashael swears that a dried pepperoni stick the men shared with them came the closest to what we understand to be the spirit of umami.

"It's as if they have some deeper understanding of the true pleasures of life," Yabbashael said after one visit to Hastings Creek, prompting an unheeded warning from Rachmiel: "Nothing good has ever come of romanticizing the downtrodden."

Towards the end of our first month, Elyon had a particularly bad day at school. When Ms. W. asked Stephan about Hamlet's indecisiveness, Elyon quoted the famous soliloquy almost in its entirety. Stephan was set upon on the way home by some future captains of industry regurgitating their bastardized brand of poetry. "Slings and arrows of outrageous faggotyness!" "To be a fucking geek or not to be a fucking geek!" and, perhaps the worst, "To sleep, perchance to wet my bed!"

"Ms. W. cut me off at 'conscience doth make cowards of us all,'" Elyon told us later behind the Wadsworths' carport as we took turns holding Jason's gym shirt to Stephan's nose and forehead to stanch the flow of blood and tears and tried to concoct a story for Stephan to tell his parents. Plain clumsiness wasn't going to help with this one. Zachriel gently cautioned that no one likes a show-off, while Barman couldn't resist dispensing some advice: "The cool answer would've been: 'What is existential angst, Alex?'" Like his avatar Leo Jr. Barman was a fan of *Jeopardy!*

Although none of us was having as hard a time as Elyon in the guise of the hapless Stephan, Arcadia Court was not exactly living up to its name. Yes, from the ravine behind our houses we could hear fern song, the endlessly unfurling fronds in the ceaseless rain. But beyond that, the equally ceaseless whine of power tools as farther up the mountainside residents sought to improve the value of their lots. From the Wadsworths' came a constant muted stench, the distinct whiff of unhappiness, and next door, from the Costellos', often the smell of scorched fish sticks and Leo Jr.'s mother singing, off-key, something about *sistahs doin' it for themselves.*

Barman, as Leo Jr., had adjusted most easily to life as a suburban teenager. Skateboard under one arm, fingers casually pinching a "spliff," revelling in the role of free spirit. "The

Dude abides with me," Barman liked saying—quoting from a Hollywood movie that had recently achieved cult status— amusing us all with the double entendre. "Nice guy, that Leo Jr." was what everyone invariably said.

Jason was a nice guy now, too, thanks to Yabbashael, but this only gave people more cause for suspicion. "Why isn't The Wad acting like a wad?" students asked, and gave him wider berth than usual, while the teachers continued to watch him out of the corners of their eyes.

Jessica's formerly papery skin shone, and curves appeared in places where before there had been alarming concavity. The boys were paying attention in the cafeteria and around her locker, although some kept their distance on account of her being The Wad's sister. The girls were a different matter. A tiny curly-haired warlord named Montana puffed out her cheeks and told her posse: "If she doesn't stop stuffing her face she'll end up like that blimp in *Precious: Based on the Novel Push by Sapphire.*"

"Well, you know how girls can be," Zachriel said.

"In fact," said Rachmiel, uncharacteristically snappy, "I don't."

It turned out that Bash, who had a fine tenor and could dance, had been cast as Judas Iscariot in the school's spring production of *Jesus Christ Superstar* before we'd appeared on the scene. His role made the rest of us nervous, but Zachriel had begun to admire Tim Rice and Sir Andrew's sympathetic view of the betrayer. "Besides," said Zachriel, "he gets all the best songs."

During the day we did our best to avoid each other as our social hierarchies dictated, but at night we lay in our beds in welcome darkness and communicated again without the boundaries of language. Speaking in tongues without need of tongues, bodiless once more.

On the ceiling of Stephan's bedroom was a glow-in-the-dark solar system, the North Star peeling away. On the wall of Leo Jr.'s room, posters from *Pirates of the Caribbean: Dead Man's Chest*. Beside Jason's pillow, a plush dolphin and an oversized neon-pink hedgehog won at the previous summer's PNE and hidden away under the bed each morning.

"How is this really different from texting?" Zachriel asked one night. Zachriel was the only one of us who'd taken to social media.

"It's different in spirit," Barman said, "and, besides, there's no need for opposable thumbs."

For some of us, high school was shaping up to be a regular pit of Acheron. ("The hue of dungeons and the scowl of night," quoth Elyon, who was finding solace in Shakespeare despite the earlier classroom misadventure.) Only ten more days to go before spring break. We began to think in terms of miracles.

How much easier it had been for Mohammed and Siddhartha, not to mention the Christ, who did not have to wander the earth incognito. "If only we could smite just a little to blow off some steam," Elyon said.

"I love that word, *smite*," Yabbashael said.

"You *guys*," Rachmiel told them, "go to sleep."

It's true we could have materialized as ravens or, in the spirit of humility, earthworms. But then how could we have partaken of all that was available to the human senses? In times past our kind have appeared as griffins or lightning or even in the form we've been represented in over the ages, luxuriously robed, or nude with dimpled flesh, wings either terrible or elegant— Masaccio's sword-wielding avenger, Bloch's pallid ectomorph, Melozzo's curly-haired candy-box creatures. But there is something too attention-getting about those guises. Something altogether beside the point.

Soon after we left Arcadia Court a giant sea tortoise, purportedly thousands of years old, appeared several blocks over on another cul-de-sac, carrying on his back a lost schoolgirl from Japan. A miracle that was quickly covered up, as it seemed it wasn't miracles these people wanted.

And while we inhabited their bodies, Bashaar, Stephan, Leo Jr., Jason, and Jessica, the children of Arcadia Court, partook of a heaven-sent dreamless sleep. There were times, we admit, that we envied them.

Stephan didn't leave the house the whole week of spring break, and when he finally emerged we almost didn't recognize him. Gone were the too-short sweatpants and checked shirts and white socks; gone were the duct-taped glasses. In their place, oversized jeans, black hoodie, and red-framed Soulja Boy sunglasses. (Gone too was approximately $500 from the university savings his superstitious parents kept hidden in a jade Fortune Vase in the pantry behind tins of water chestnuts.) When we converged on him, Stephan simply raised a hand and said, "Word."

He failed a math test that week, the first of many, and when called on in English or Socials he'd say things like, "Existential angst, man," ignoring meaningful pokes from Leo Jr. ("Stephan's so *random*," his male classmates said approvingly, so we could only conclude this was a good thing, this doing poorly in school and waxing random.)

Stephan spent much of this time on multiplayer role-playing games online. By all accounts he was a master at *World of Warcraft: Realm of Cocytus*, "smiting the enemy," who consisted of a new kind of Wyrm and Nephilim—a.k.a. "those douche-bags," according to the faux-hawk kid. (Barman scoffed at how the game developers stole so readily from ur-biblical sources. "*Nephilim*. They have no idea what they're dealing with. No wonder Elyon has their number.")

We soon heard reports that Stephan was hacking for his classmates. His new admirers were his old adversaries, pimply boys with too much pocket money who took to intoning "S'mite" to each other in greeting.

Yabbashael and Barman tried to talk sense into Elyon one afternoon in the Choo family's backyard. "You two should talk," Elyon said, eyes non-existent behind those disconcerting lenses, avoiding directly addressing Barman. "*His* guy was already cool, and *your* guy is an armoured vehicle." Barman asked if this was all some kind of twisted revenge scenario, but Elyon only said, "By the time we leave, Stephan will be *made*."

On an early April morning Stephan's parents slowly chewed and swallowed their shame dumplings and visited the school counsellor, shuffling along the main hall of Elysium Heights Secondary, past the glass-fronted trophy case filled with testaments to young male and female physical prowess, their son strutting behind them.

Stephan's ancient grandmother, who lived in the basement suite of the family home, had been making twice-daily offerings to Kwan Yin, the Bodhisattva of compassion, on her small Buddhist shrine. Zachriel saw her that day walking along the edge of the ravine behind Arcadia Court, bending painfully to tug up freshly blooming false Solomon's seal and collect choice pine cones. The moist-earth aroma, Zachriel said, was almost indecent. Nearby, on a dying Douglas fir, a pileated woodpecker let loose with a maniacal laugh and went back to his drumming. Stephan's grandmother raised her tortoise face and (Zachriel swore on Bashaar's *JC Superstar* script, rolled up in his back pocket) echoed that lunatic laughter right back at the bird.

What karmic justice, she might have been thinking, had led her to be a ninety-six-year-old woman traipsing through the rainforest at the edge of the world, mother to an aging son whose own child had lost all sense of filial piety?

We couldn't help but wonder how was it that we could be drawn to an object, that a pair of sneakers dangling from a telephone wire, the rubber curling back from the heels, could break our hearts, yet we felt so little for the suffering of these parents?

That same day, Jessica's mother steered her to the couch when she came home in a shirt two sizes smaller than the one she'd left the house wearing and tried to engage her in a heart-to-heart about birth control, sexually transmitted diseases, and dressing like a harlot—although the word she used was "slut." We found it both interesting and disturbing that people's attitudes towards women and their bodies had changed so little since the days of Nebuchadnezzar II. ("The Madonna/whore dichotomy is so tired," sighed Barman.)

This was Jessica's opportunity to tell her mother she loved her and that she was looking forward to being guided through womanhood by her sagacity. Instead, she turned her head, looked pointedly at her own chipped nail polish, and sighed dramatically.

"I don't know what got into me," Rachmiel told us afterwards. "I wanted to put my arms around her, tell her that human life is too short, too precious to spend it endlessly worrying about things we cannot change, and that I could take care of myself, but she was just so—"

"Irritating?" asked Yabbashael.

We couldn't help nodding in compadreship; we all had mothers now. Maryam, Um Isa, Our Lady of Sorrows, Panayia, Kali, forgive us.

For a few weeks that spring, mounds of debris floating in the lower waterways of the North Shore spontaneously exploded—fiery islets of discarded tires tangled with fast-food clamshells and wrappers, plastic bottles, beer cans, undergarments, and the occasional lone sneaker drifted along the mountain creeks. The sight, at least at night, was disconcertingly lovely.

Several freight cars had jumped the tracks in the CN rail yard, the derailment spilling 41,000 litres of corrosive sodium hydroxide. Someone, it was reported, had tampered with a manual switch. (The same cast of individual, Elyon noted with disdain, who a week earlier had beaten three peacocks dead with a tire iron in Stanley Park.)

The contamination gave the parents of Arcadia Court another reason to forbid their children to go near Hastings Creek or its tributaries. The few Dolly Varden and steelhead still left in the creeks floated by, ulcerated bellies up. Some construction workers near Baird Road found a young bobcat, its whiskers and facial fur eaten away, mewling blindly beside its dead mother under a semi-completed kitchen extension. Domesticated animals were kept inside or tethered in yards. Someone, somewhere, was investigating.

The news media said this caustic substance smelled like absolutely nothing—a chemical that is impossible to detect with human senses.

Towards late April, Jessica began consorting with an older boy, a certain Cullen, who rode a coveted make of British motorcycle. Sullen Cullen, Barman nicknamed him, after his propensity for moping about, leaning against his bike with his head in a copy of Rilke's *Letters to a Young Poet* when Jessica wasn't with him.

And so Rachmiel stopped talking to the rest of us in public while Jessica was busy romancing Cullen, but still joined our nocturnal debriefings. Unlike Elyon. Stephan was by then making "good coin" cracking codices for his classmates, and Elyon didn't want to be privy to our "sanctimonious brand of negativity." Stephan took to wearing bulky jewellery and talking in rhyme with his escort of swaggering boys whose ears were stopped up with neon buds at all times.

Yabbashael and Barman were by then enjoying themselves as Jason and Leo Jr. and spent much of their free time visiting the Three Wise Men of Hastings Creek: Gary, Lubbock, and Sweeney. None of them were as old as they'd initially appeared. They'd been prematurely aged by an adult life spent living rough and not always by choice. Yabbashael was certain— following an afternoon of warm beer and discussions about the philosophy of shopping-cart racing—they were zeroing in on the ne plus ultra of human experience.

Our carnal senses had also fully awakened by then. Jason was "spanking the monkey" so often that Yabbashael complained Jason's foreskin looked—and felt—like tender-ized minute steak. Leo gave and got his first hickey, although Barman was oddly bashful when asked with whom. Jessica and Cullen were spotted, more than once, coming out of the Wadsworths' laundry room, sheets of fabric softener clinging to their dishevelled hair. Rachmiel seemed to have taken a vow of silence about the affair and shared nothing with the rest of us during our after-hours conversations.

Bashaar was busy with the school's rock opera preparations

at that point. Each evening after rehearsal, in the encroaching darkness outside the gymnasium, the two grade ten girls who played Mary and Mary, and a grade eleven girl from the chorus, would take turns administering oral sex to Bash with lipstick-thickened, smoky mouths. ("Rainbow party," Zachriel told us, and in a tone of reverence up to then reserved for Psalm 19, New International Version, tried to describe the sensation. One of the Marys evidently swallowed, but Zachriel couldn't recall which.)

It was after one particularly long rehearsal that they were interrupted by a couple of the radicalized Islamic youth. As the girls scrambled to their feet and vanished into the night, Bash zipped himself up unhurriedly and said, "Ma sha' Allah," attempting to be polite.

One of the young men fingered his sparse beard and asked, equally politely, whether Bash had decided to drop the blasphemous line from the song "Superstar." (The one questioning whether Mohammed could move a mountain, or whether he simply had a good publicist.) The way Bash's interlocutor put it, it sounded more like a threat than an entreaty, especially since his silent colleague kept smacking his fist into his palm to punctuate the request. We wonder now, after everything, what would have happened if Bash had revealed he was inhabited by a messenger sent by the same Jibrail who had delivered the Qur'an to their prophet. Would they have believed him, laughed, or condemned him on the spot for blasphemy?

Why, they appeared to genuinely want to know, would Bashaar waste his time with these infidel females when seventy-two virgins awaited him in paradise?

"I wanted to disabuse them of their ill-conceived notions of martyrdom right then and there," Zachriel would later claim, almost five years to the day we left Arcadia Court, when a defaced For Sale sign went up on the Khan family's front lawn and the street was a jumble of yellow police tape, "but I just couldn't stop thinking about those Marys. Their lips. Their tongues."

By then we knew the body inevitably betrayed the mind.

Are we good? The question is often asked. We transcend the notion of good or bad as understood in the human sense. We simply *are*. An idea difficult to grasp, like the workings of the Hadron Collider or why the caged bird sings. The novelist Philip Pullman came closest to understanding the complexity of our kind with Balthamos and Baruch in his *Amber Spyglass*. ("Ironic that it took an atheist to get it right," Barman said. Barman had, by then, nailed the concept.)

The afternoon Leo Jr. died and was reborn and our days at Arcadia Court became numbered was a fine Saturday in late May. Gary and Lubbock had convinced Sweeney that Jason and Leo Jr. were spiritually primed to undertake their first shopping-cart race. A picture of what happened that day has been pieced together from Yabbashael, Barman, and Rachmiel's separate accounts.

In the parking lot of Save-On Foods ("Highest percentage of carts without wonky wheels, bar none," said Gary), Sweeney instructed the boys to approach the carts as if they were wild stallions and try to sense which ones spoke to them. Lubbock said, "Forget that farting around, just grab one and let's get going." An argument broke out but was quickly resolved when Leo Jr. grabbed a cart and threw himself across the parking lot, "popping a wheelie," and landed hard on his backside while the men laughed and coughed and forgot what they'd been raging about moments before.

They hefted hunks of concrete into their shopping carts at

a nearby demolition site, and, all five carts balanced, wheels true, they rattled towards Mountain Highway. After some last-minute adjustments and a reminder to use the inside left foot as a brake, the men and boys howled down the winding road, motorized vehicles honking and veering around them. "The eighteen seconds or so before I blacked out were the most thrilling of my human life," Barman told us later.

According to Yabbashael, Barman (that is, Leo Jr.) went screaming out ahead, perhaps emboldened by his skateboarding expertise, misjudged the first curve, and flew several metres into the scrub off the side of the road. Gary administered mouth-to-mouth even though Leo Jr. had no pulse. Barman later told us a tunnel of white light beckoned to Leo Jr., but something (the yeasty taste of stale beer mixed with damp tobacco strands?) pulled him back.

Heady with stirred-up testosterone, Jason and Leo Jr. made for Hastings Creek after they bid the cart racers goodbye and promised to make another run the next day. What met them was a sight Barman described as "something out of the Apocalypse of John the Divine."

Amidst crushed ferns a two-headed beast writhed, while the sound of trumpets sundered the welkin. On the blast of the seventh, they perceived "a woman clothed with the sun, the moon, and the stars, and Satan cast down to earth."

Barman insists to this day that it was a trick of filtered light and shadow created by the trees that led to the visual confusion, and that the sound of trumpets was thunder preceding a storm. To Barman's embarrassment they'd stumbled onto a private scene of two young people in the thrall of carnal exuberance. (Some of us believe what occurred there by the creek was a result of Yabbashael's taking the protector role of Jason as "big" brother too seriously.)

Jason heaved up a large, muddy stone from the side of the creek while Leo Jr. stood by as if in a trance. He brought the stone down on the back of the beast, at which point a scream cleared the air. Jessica lay under a seemingly lifeless Cullen as blood ran into his ponytail from a fissure in his neck. Her eyes, Barman recalls, were terrible, like the maw of a deep-sea dweller. When she spoke, it was in the inner voice of Rachmiel, who said, as if it cost everything Rachmiel had to give, "May the God forgive you." The sky thundered again as the deluge started and Jessica struggled back into her clothes.

The rest happened quickly. An ambulance was fetched, a tale concocted. Lubbock, Gary, and Sweeney, swearing their innocence, indignant spittle flying, were arrested by the end of the day. Leo Jr. took the extra keys to the Costellos' Ford Escape, and—with only eighteen months of payments remaining—totalled the front end driving into the side of a Dairy Queen. Jason went into his bedroom and refused to come out for three days, almost as comatose as Cullen himself. (Yabbashael planned to remain in self-exile for forty days and forty nights until Barman pointed out that Yabbashael was not the Christ.)

Amidst all this drama, Bashaar had his star turn in the school musical, which, according to the local weeklies, was a hit, and Stephan was suspended and threatened with repeating grade eight.

"So what." Elyon shrugged. "He's never had this much fun in his life." The Choo house visibly sagged in on itself as his parents shuffled downcast from room to room. Stephan's grandmother no longer gathered offerings but sat in front of the basement television set watching Fox News.

Leo Jr.'s neck brace stayed on for almost three weeks, and to this day his right hand is not as mobile as his left due to the manner in which the broken bones fused.

Even now, so many years on, we take pains to remind each other of what Augustine once said: "*Angelus est nomen offici*," which Barman suggests translating as, "'Angel' is the name of the office."

In other words, it's our *job*, not who we *are*. We mention this as a fact, not as a kind of apologia.

Jessica skipped school regularly to visit the hospitalized Cullen, who was hooked up to all manner of medical equipment in Lions Gate Hospital's ICU, and unresponsive. She held his hand for hours every day. (Once, when he blinked and appeared to part his lips, his mother said, "She's an angel of mercy!" before leaving the room, crying. Rachmiel admitted praying for intervention from St. Jude. But did Rachmiel ask for a miracle? We think not.)

In mid-June, Bashaar was at the Shoppers Drug Mart buying condoms when he spotted Jessica pulling a pregnancy kit from a shelf. Bash slid up behind her and whispered, "You weren't going to tell us, were you?" She was so startled she dropped the Very-Berry Slurpee she was carrying in her other hand, splashing them both with what looked like clotted blood.

After everything that had happened, at last a true crisis was upon us, one that we could not simply turn the other cheek on and hope for the best.

Even Elyon joined us as we debated late into the night whether to destroy the child or both mother and child—deep within us stirred and rumbled the fear of waking the slumbering Nephilim. Rachmiel argued, in the end effectively, that the warlike giants of old were the spawn of rogue angels and mortal women, not of angels and mortal men, so we agreed to stay our hands.

No one used the word *smite*. Not once. Not even Elyon.

The summons that came from Gabriel that night was firm and unequivocal. We were recalled from earth with no time to say our goodbyes.

We took our shameful leave as day dawned on Arcadia Court, all but Rachmiel, who made a choice one of our kind has seldom made, and not without enormous sacrifice. Jessica's small, moon-white face was pressed to the Wadsworths' bay window as if there were something to see besides a blue, cloudless sky. Zachriel wrote a message across the firmament in white wisps: *Errare humanum est. Perseverare diabolicum.* He meant it kindly.

Our mission aborted, we took sensory experiences with us as if we were junior entomologists pinning to a corkboard butterfly specimens snuffed out with ethyl acetate. But what we left behind is what we remember most vividly. One thing we all agree on: the much-vaunted human heart is just a wayward muscle.

Not long after we left, young Stephan Choo was found face down in Hastings Creek near the place where Cullen had sustained his injury. His suicide note remains hidden, to this day, in a jade Fortune Vase in his parents' pantry. Six months later, on the adoption papers Jessica Wadsworth signed, her premature daughter bore the name Stephanie in complicated and guilty tribute. Cullen emerged from his coma with no further interest in either Rilke or Jessica and her predicament. We could have told her so.

It took a while, years in fact, but Bashaar eventually succumbed to the enticements of his patient recruiters. The Khan family's garage became a repository of Kemira GrowHow fertilizer and pallets of nail-polish remover. Local authorities were tipped off. The rest was all dutifully reported in the media, including Bashaar's bewildered parents claiming they believed the supplies were for their son's year-end biochemistry project at SFU, their dark eyes a haunting. YouTube footage of the much younger and still beardless "home-grown terrorist" dancing on the stage of Elysium Heights Secondary's gymnasium singing "Strange Thing Mystifying" went viral.

The Wad carried on being a wad.

As for Leo Jr., he turned out fine. Like his father he became a forensic accountant. He auditioned for *Jeopardy!* once while on a business trip to Atlanta, but after the eighteen-month waiting period lapsed, simply forgot about it. We try not to judge, but we had imagined a life of more freedom for him, perhaps as a first AD for local film productions or a tennis coach. In another era he could have joined a travelling circus. But he abides.

And us? We have a special dispensation to watch over Jessica's child, even though we know she is more than capable of taking care of herself.

On our phantom tongues the taste of humanity lingers. But something else as well. The fifth taste?

That thing that eludes us still.

BETTER LIVING THROUGH PLASTIC EXPLOSIVES

The act of naming is the great and solemn consolation of mankind.

—ELIAS CANETTI, *THE AGONY OF FLIES*

SKULLBLAST

Wisteria hangs over the eaves like clumps of ghostly grapes. Euphorbia's pale blooms billow like sea froth. Blood grass twists upward, knifing the air, while underground its roots go berserk, goosing everything in their path. A magnolia, impatient with vulvic flesh, erupts in front of the living-room window. The recovering terrorist—holding a watering can filled with equal parts fish fertilizer and water, paisley gloves right up over her freckled forearms, a straw hat with its big brim shading her eyes, old tennis shoes speckled with dew—moves through her front garden. Her face, she tells herself, like a Zen koan. The look of one lip smiling.

A car shoots down the street too fast, a fifteen-year-old future ex-con at the wheel, tires squealing as he turns the corner onto Victoria, actually *burning rubber*, as it's called, and the recovering terrorist drops her watering can. Reeking fish fertilizer slops onto her sneakers.

She has written letters to city hall requesting a traffic circle (*a speed retardant*, as it's called, putting her in mind of the large, soft boy with slivered moons of dirt under his fingernails who shuffled around in a slow-moving cloud at the back of her third-grade classroom before being taken away to wherever children like that were taken away to back then). She has circulated a petition that her neighbours have eagerly signed. They all have small children and animals, as does the recovering terrorist. They are teachers and enviropreneurs and directors of small NGOs that help build medical facilities in developing countries. They've promised to fill the traffic circle with indigenous flora, promised to guard against graffiti, to ensure it doesn't become a dumpsite for used condoms, syringes, Twizzler wrappers, and the inevitable orphaned muffler. But the city just keeps putting them off, citing a litany of bureaucratic impediments. The recovering terrorist has telephoned, again and again. She's been told, *red tape red tape red tape red tape*. She's said, "Look, it's a traffic circle, *a speed retardant* we're asking for here, not a water filtration plant."

The recovering terrorist has a name that sounds like fresh fruit, an ingénue of a name. Girl terrorists all seem to have perky names—Squeaky, Patty, Julie—as if they can't quite take themselves seriously enough. When she first stood up at group, about three years ago, and said, "My name is —— and I am a terrorist," she felt none of the relief the small ad in the *Georgia Straight* had assured her she'd be flooded with.

As the others set their coffee cups down between their feet

and clapped supportively (one guy, who she later would come to know as Dieter, even whistled through four fingers wolf-style), she felt like a small-town beauty contestant—Miss Chilliwack promising to end global warming, sectarian strife, and escalating movie theatre prices before the end of her reign. Not like someone who had once burned down a house to bring a petty capitalist to his knees. She kept on going to the meetings, though. There was something reassuring about the camaraderie, a single-mindedness of purpose she hadn't felt since that night almost twenty years ago when her life cleaved in two.

In the local paper this morning there was a letter to the editor from a Port Moody woman whose daughter had been hit by a car right in front of her house on a quiet residential street. The girl was so small she had rolled out the other side and lay curled like a shrimp. Her teeth were embedded in the roof of her mouth, in the pouches of her cheeks, scattered on the road like a handful of Chiclets. The car just kept on going. *What kind of person*—the mother asked.

The recovering terrorist slips off a glove and squeezes a few black aphids between her thumb and forefinger, their bodies barely yielding before that satisfying pop and squelch. She thinks about issuing a threat, some sort of ultimatum, targeting the mayor's office. Her heart rate nearly doubles at the thought, and desire, no, *need*, swells her throat, and she feels as if she's choking. Something in her veins actually slithers. *I'm jonesing for a Fudgsicle*, her son said the other day, and how they'd laughed. *Jonesing*. What does he know about jonesing? She stumbles up the front steps into the house and is blinded by the sudden shift from sunlit yard to windowless front hall. Light blemishes explode across her retinas. When she reaches the telephone she punches the speed-dial, hoping Dieter will answer.

Dieter is trying to picture Tim with an AK-47. Lucy is trying to picture Tim and Dieter on a date. She listens to Dieter splutter loudly in disbelief as a woman at the next café table makes a show of dragging her chair away from them.

"He's so *verklemmt*, I can't stand it," Dieter says. Every time Lucy and Dieter meet, Dieter obsesses about how much he hates Tim, to the point where Lucy has begun to suspect Dieter is actually attracted to Tim but can't admit it. Because Dieter likes men with moral fibre and a supple sense of humour, and Tim, from the evidence they've seen, gets what little fibre he has from a cereal box, and his idea of funny begins and ends with a knock-knock joke. (*Dwayne the bathtub, I'm dwowning!*)

"*You* know," Dieter says, putting his hands around his throat and gagging like a cat processing an enormous hairball.

The waiter comes by and tells them the coffee of the day is a Brazilian Go-go Carnival, but organic, fair-trade, shade-grown Brazilian, not rainforest-stripping, parrot-habitat-destroying, barefoot-peasant-exploiting Brazilian, therefore explaining its $5.95-a-cup price tag. This sets Dieter off again.

"And a *Brazilian* businessman. Who the fuck cares?"

This is the real sticking point, the one Lucy agrees with. *Think globally, act locally.* It's just too easy to hie off to mainland China with your Gap khakis rolled around a *Free Tibet!!* banner in your backpack, while crack-addicted babies gnaw on french fries and stare listlessly from strollers parked outside the Money Mart ("Real People. Real Cash.") right here on Commercial Drive. For Lucy it always comes down to the babies, and soon she's holding back Lollapalooza-sized tears that threaten to start smashing guitars all over the stage of her face.

If Tim had been trying to save babies, wide-faced, velvet-lashed Brazilian babies, she might even admire him a little. But she somehow can't imagine Tim—fine-boned, twitchy, *verklemmt* Tim—toting a semi-automatic and taking his turn guarding the cellar of a house in the suburbs just outside of São Paulo, peeing into an Orangina bottle, eating without a knife and fork, letting a balaclava mess with his ginger hair, for the sake of babies.

"It's good for me to vent like this," Dieter says. "It keeps me under control. It scratches the itch. You"—he takes Lucy's hand, the one not playing catapult with her spoon—"you need a diversion."

"I have Bruno and Foster, you jerk. And The Hound." She launches her spoon at him and he ducks to one side. "I have my work, my garden-bitch show." She knows what he's thinking. That if she had a real diversion she wouldn't phone him with such frequency, such urgency; she wouldn't continually be so close to slipping. If she had a diversion, she wouldn't be so focused on what might happen to Foster.

But her fear is her diversion. It keeps her in check. Her fear is state-of-the-art titanium crampons on the frozen icefall that has for so long been her life.

SUCKER PUNCH

The recovering terrorist sits on her front steps watching her husband assemble their son's new unicycle. The boy is so excited he starts clutching at himself as if he has to go to the bathroom. "Do you have to go the bathroom?" she calls out, but he ignores her. And her heart does a funny thing. It flops over in her chest like a fish gasping on a dock.

The boy, at age seven, has decided to master every form of wheeled transport known to mankind. His skateboard and scooter and bike are covered with Pokémon stickers, and the boy never tires of explaining how the fierce little creatures evolve and what weapons they have (wake-up slap, mean look, skull blast, hyper voice, Zen headbutt, poison jab, sucker punch, fury attack, gunk shot, aurora beam, worry seed, tail whip, drill peck, lava plume, stun spore—the list of moves is seemingly without end) and the number of "health points" lost with each assault. The one he likes best has blazing fur and can immolate everything in its path. Their dog is named after Houndoom, a fire-breathing horned beast with an eerie howl. The only thing their aging dachshund shares with her namesake is her weird yowling bark.

The unicycle is upright and there goes the boy, swaying from side to side but somehow staying aloft. Her husband runs alongside and turns his head to grin back at her and almost trips over an abandoned Safeway shopping cart that's angled across the sidewalk, tipping into the gutter. The boy keeps on going, Houndoom at his heels, yelling something that sounds like "Sludge bomb!" before pulling a wet and blobby thing from his pocket and hurling it into the street while her husband clutches his shin and yells, "Fuck!"

"Be careful!" she calls after her son. There's a hitch in her throat and it comes out sounding like carfool. Be careful. Her lame mantra, her new default middle name.

"Gardening is like warfare and it's time for you to call in the troops," The Gardening Dame tells her caller, Sue from Ladner. "Fly parasites, green lacewing, convergent lady beetles—that's teenaged ladybugs, they're hot for aphids—and parasitic nematodes, basically little worms that burrow into grubs and weevils *Alien*-like, stopping them in their tracks before they can take down your tomatoes and basil."

Sue from Ladner: "I've heard Chinese praying mantis is a good predator."

The Gardening Dame: "Well, they're amusing to watch, but a little show-offy relative to their effectiveness. Think Owen Wilson versus Jackie Chan in *Shanghai Knights*."

You weren't a true terrorist unless you were willing to risk hurting the innocent to achieve your goals. This is the kind of thing they debated at group as they stood around eating Peek Freans and drinking instant coffee during the break, the coffee whitener's oily sheen creating little rainbows in their cups.

One guy at group had talked about money all the time. Only he called it "moolah." He had also reminisced about "five-finger discounts" and boasted that he'd never—*ever*—paid for a meal or rent. "That's what girlfriends are for," he'd said, elbowing Dieter in the ribs. "Oops, *you* wouldn't know." They changed locations twice on the sly before they managed to shake him. Dieter admitted he'd gotten a charge out of that bit of clandestine business, at which Tim rolled his eyes. "What?" Dieter said, his own eyes uncanny behind his industrial-strength lenses. "I like secrets. Is that all of a sudden a crime?" The facilitator, Angelina, told them they were lucky they weren't in her first group, where there'd been a pro-lifer who kept quoting *Horton Hears a Who!* in a squeaky little voice: "A person's a person, no matter how small."

Now they have a saying, "It's not about the moolah." The one thing they are not is mercenary.

What Lucy's been thinking lately: Was there really any difference between financial reward and the services of seventy virgins (give or take a few) spread-eagled on a cloud awaiting a martyr in paradise? None that she could see.

When Angelina gave them all T-shirts at Christmas that read *It's not about the moolah*, every single one of them went silent and then mushy, hugging one other, some crying, Dieter, glasses on floor, so hard that tears leaked from between his fingers, something Lucy had only ever seen before in cartoons.

ZEN HEADBUTT

The recovering terrorist stands at a counter on the second floor of City Hall waiting to speak with a man who has to press his left thumb against a hole in his throat in order to talk, as if he's pushing a button on an intercom. His voice comes out filtered, almost electronic sounding, like the Pixar people's concept of a robotic voice. The boy has been watching from a chair in the open waiting area with too much interest. He jams a thumb against his throat and mouths something she can't make out. *Beam me up, Scotty*, she thinks, and laughs, which is a mistake because her son notices, so she tries to look stern.

She loves this crazy kid so much it actually physically hurts. This love does devastating things to her intestines that only something like listeriosis generally does to saner people. Or is she confusing love with fear? For all her past-life bravado, she finally understands what it means to be willing to die for something, or rather, someone. He is her ur-text, her Gospels, her Koran.

In a nearby cubicle, voices are engaged in a heated negotiation involving explosive black powder, the volume and quantity of semi-automatic gunshots, and squib hits. Plenty of squib hits. "Opening a fire hydrant costs *how* much?" a male voice whimpers. "But this is a *Canadian* film." The bureaucrat's response is *sotto voce*. In addition to road, sewage, and garbage issues, the Engineering Department handles filming permits, the city's big cash cow.

"I will not submit my request by phone, because I've already done that. I've been calling your department for weeks," the recovering terrorist says, speaking louder than she should, as if the man in front of her is missing his eardrums rather than his larynx. She's arguing with a guy who has no voice box, albeit a guy using his disability as an excuse to be an asshole. He finally concedes to set up a meeting with the administrator in charge of traffic calming measures. The recovering terrorist glances at the appointment slip he hands her. "July 18! That's more than a month away. By then—" By then what? Will she be able to hold out that long without slipping through a crack?

The man presses his thumb to his throat and looks past her. "Next."

Outside, on the City Hall tower, the four faces of the neon clock all show an entirely different time. It's been this way for years. This is *a city on the edge*, as it's called, a city on the edge of an idea. Maybe the idea that time is relative?

"So was that guy a cyborg or what?" her son asks as they make their way down the worn marble stairs to the lobby, and she realizes from his expression that he's serious. The recovering terrorist takes the opportunity to launch into a lecture about the dangers of smoking. She's segueing rather nicely from tobacco to crack when her son stops and drops her hand. "But what if someone just stabbed a stick into his throat? Like a maniac? What if it's not his fault!?" He looks furious. "What if someone did that to you?!" In his face she thinks she can see the man he'll become. But where will his inchoate sense of injustice lead him?

It's 4:00, it's 6:18, it's 1:45, it's almost midnight. It's getting late.

When he was younger the boy was always wanting to know what something was called, like all fledgling humans, from Adam and Enkidu to Kaspar Hauser on down. Manhole covers, squirrels, body parts, graffiti, discarded condoms, black-eyed Susans, facial deformities on fellow passengers riding the No. 20 bus. That got name? That got name? Easy enough until he pointed to something unnameable. That got name? My face? Eyes? No, he howled, *that!* almost poking her eye out. Eyelashes? Iris? Pupil? But he became inconsolable, a cartoon parody of toddler rage.

It was only later, lying in bed that night, that she began to wonder. Had he meant her soul?

Now his hunger for naming is satiated with his trading cards, hundreds upon hundreds of names and attributes. Vulpix, Nidorino, Pikachu, Torterra, Weezing, Lickitung, Steelix, Uxie, Dusknoir, Deoxys, Gligar, Slugma, the latter's body made of lava so it can't stop moving or it will cool and harden. A favourite of the boy's. Somewhere in Toyko's Nihonbashi district there is a name factory, no doubt, where adult men and women with orange hair, wearing T-shirts with impossibly cute slogans, brainstorm all day for characters' names while sipping bubble tea through straws and smoking thin brown Indian cigarettes.

The other day a card was lying face up on the side of the bathtub, Houndoom's teeth marks on it. Typhlosion, a creature with a collar of flame that looks like a cross between Godzilla and a skunk. Special moves: Flamethrower, Lava Plume, Eruption. "Typhlosion ignites fire blasts by rubbing its hairs against one another. It uses the resulting heat haze to hide itself. Anything touching it while it is aroused will be up in flames instantly." This is the most evolved Pokémon of its kind.

"Diatomaceous earth is pretty effective," The Gardening Dame tells her caller. "Millions of years ago little marine creatures died out just so we could use their skeletons to kill slugs. Crawling over the stuff is like crawling through ground glass."

Brian from Quesnel: "Isn't that unnecessarily barbaric?"

The Gardening Dame: "You could do what I do and go out in the night with a miner's light strapped to your head and track them down one by one, pour salt on them, and watch them sizzle and hiss."

Brian from Quesnel: "That's sick."

The Gardening Dame: "An eye for an eye, *as they say*, a tooth for a tooth."

WAKE-UP SLAP

Every night at a certain hour the recovering terrorist can feel her fear rising like a reeking tidal backwash, and here it comes now, lugging kelp and dead crabs onto the shore. At night she is never alone. These particles that move through the air, the ones that appear as large and small spots in front of your eyes, these must be the constituents of hell.

There is the girl in her open coffin, not like it was at the funeral. But that's the only difference. There is the pastor, disconcertingly cheerful, and the family. The church is like a big A-frame cabin. Pale wood beams arch gently up, joining at the point where the ceiling pierces the sky. *The heavens*, as it's called.

The pastor turns his palms upward as if checking for rain. "Anna has been transported from a scene of pain and sorrow to a land that knows no pain. God said, 'Well done, Anna, you passed the test, come home.'" The young voices in the choir, schoolchildren, sing of the Lord coming to gather his jewels.

Behind the recovering terrorist a woman is whispering loudly, "Anna was fascinated with Heaven and could not, could *not*, wait for the Second Coming. She said, 'Mommy, I want to go home to be with Jesus.' And her mother said, 'Don't you want to stay here with Mommy and Daddy?'" Teary sighs of understanding from the surrounding pews. The pastor says, "We pray for the person, or persons, responsible for this act."

Whatever this is called, it's not a dream.

Her co-conspirators were furious that she'd gone to the funeral. "Are you insane?" hissed Damien—a man, no, a beautiful boy really, whose cock only six days earlier she had held in her mouth—before disappearing from her life forever. She heard that he was in Dawson City or Kathmandu—like Elvis there were sightings for years and then nothing. One by one the others disappeared as well. Dissolving, so it seemed, into mist, but resurfacing south of the border and eventually apprehended for other crimes, bigger, more glamorous ones, yet not nearly so terrible. She was the only one with collateral damage to her credit. And yet here she is, *hiding in plain sight*, as it's called.

Poor, virginal Leonard, with his sense of aggrievement— Capt. Elmer Fudd, they called him, because of his stutter— became a prison poet, the most productive time of his life, he told *Rolling Stone*. Since he got out, nothing, but he still saw himself "as a fundamentally good person." Carmen posed for Annie Leibovitz, pregnant, naked, and holding a Pancor Jackhammer across her breasts and fruited belly, a daisy sprouting from the gun's muzzle. This was before making the FBI's most-wanted list a second time. Regan and Gerry, always the clowns, had tried to get a mock reality show called *Urban Guerrilla* off the ground. That's what happened, you did your time and you moved on. It must be a colossal relief, she thinks, something that doesn't compute in her cosmology.

Every so often in the early years, there were rumours of a "sixth member." But her name had never come up.

The early-summer heat wave is getting to everyone at group. That and the *woof* of decaying fish from the back-alley bin of the Indonesian restaurant next door to their meeting space. Oppressing everyone, that is, except Lucy, who's energized as she confesses her imagined assault on City Hall. How she envisions it: like the ending of a movie running on under the credits rather then dissolving to black, fantastical slo-mo destruction to a hypnotic soundtrack, something by Philip Glass or Arvo Pärt. And her right there, facing the statue of Captain Vancouver as debris falls like cleansing rain. Her blood is singing. She almost has to lick her lips, the scene is just that tasty. She tells them about how she's gone to the Vancouver Archives and looked up the blueprints, how locating the most vulnerable points of the building was like tracing the veins of a lover's arms.

There's a kind of silence for a moment, the scratching at soaked pits, the slurping of coffee, looks exchanged. Of all of them, Lucy has the strongest urges, has to work the hardest to quell that insatiable need to act or threaten to act in order to have her demands met, to inflict order. Maybe they were all just dissatisfied children who had never grown up. Angelina puts down her cup and applauds Lucy's confession, and the rest join in, but tepidly. The point is to offer support, not pass judgment, but Lucy can see that she's making them tired. Especially Dieter, who so wants to move on, to forget all this, get married to a nice man, *be normal*, as it's called. He wants what he thinks she has.

"Um, so power to the people, right on." Lucy pumps her fist in the air, trying to lighten the mood, fettered as it is by heat and stench and her own neediness. "Free Leonard Pelletier!"

"Excuse me, but that's so not funny," says Hamish-Two-Fins, the born-again native. After discovering six years ago that his great-great grandmother had been one-eighth Kitlope, of the Killer Whale clan, it's been one warrior cry after another, and a short hop from there to wannabe terrorist.

Does she know any of these people at all? These members of her "book club," as she's described her Wednesday-night outings to Bruno. Does knowing their deepest desires mean anything, does having glimpsed the rusty drip pan under their hearts entitle her to their trust? Do they really have anything in common at all? There's an elderly woman who calls herself The Wife. There's Sterling, the tree-spiker. Tim, whose well-connected daddy somehow got him back from Brazil before he even ran short of changes of pressed boxers. Molly, who'd waged a campaign of terror against her West End neighbour-hood's johns. Wing-Soo, whose story was an epic saga involving container ships, human snakes, payola, nasty landlords, and lost children. And Hamish, who's been banned from Kitamaat Village by the hereditary chief, presumably, Lucy thinks, for being annoying. Angelina is the only one among them who'd done time. She shrugged it off whenever they asked. "It was the sixties. Everyone did something."

Then there is Dieter, dear Dieter. A charter member of ACT UP, he'd taken part in a direct-action campaign in which a syringe purportedly tainted with the AIDS virus was planted tip up in the seat of a movie theatre. It was one of a chain owned by the family of the wife of the Canadian CEO of pharmaceutical giant GlaxoBioProgress. (Besides, Dieter told her he'd reasoned, they were showing *Gigli* with Ben Affleck, and anyone who would go to see that ...) But the screening that day had been the sneak preview of a children's movie. Dieter panicked and called the cops and swore off direct action for life. Among his former inner circle he's now a pariah, or The Turned Wurm, as he calls himself when he's feeling cheerful.

"What, no exegesis on Tim's latest outfit?" Lucy asks as they walk towards Waterfront station after group, Dieter uncharacteristically quiet. "I thought it was cute in a golf-daddy kind of way. No sweatshop labour involved. How do I know this? Because he confides in me."

"Do you have any idea how many die-ins I've been in with people who are now actually dead?" Dieter says. "I'm sick of going to funerals and visiting people in prison. People I love."

"If you're proposing to me, you'll have to go down on one knee."

"You want to know what I think?" Under the flashing sign of a donair shop Dieter's face blinks in and out of view. "I think you're looking for an excuse to blow something up. I think you want to be caught." The pressed meat on its rod turns slowly in the window, glistening, slick with a fatty sheen.

"Maybe I need a new sponsor," Lucy says.

"Maybe. I don't think I'm helping your spiritual growth."

Lucy can't help cracking a smile, but it feels crumbly, as if her face is a plaster mask.

"Seriously, I'm afraid I won't be able to stop you."

Up north, someone is sabotaging the natural-gas pipeline. The bomber sends almost illegible handwritten notes to the company, calling them terrorists. Lucy envies him his sense of mission. And his patience. He's given them five years to dismantle the $1.8-billion project, three months to commit. Who has five years? Who has three months? Who has the guts to be *the pot calling the kettle black*, in shoddy penmanship to boot?

DRILL PECK

The recovering terrorist deadheads bee balm in her front garden, the red-tufted joker heads strewn at her feet like carnage from the suicide bombing of a medieval fairground. Her son spins up and down the sidewalk on his unicycle trying to juggle three oranges. His dad's idea and, of course, he loves it. *Carfool.* Now he's talking about learning to juggle fire.

A car streaks by, its boom-box bass competing with the squeal of tires as it tears onto Victoria and she can't help herself, she runs after it, waving her secateurs at the dissipating exhaust. "I'll clip your skinny little balls next time!" The boy leaps from his unicycle and rolls around on the grass, screaming, "Balls! Balls!" Houndoom commences her unearthly yowling. Her husband opens the front door, still in his SpongeBob boxers. "Hey!"

"Mom said 'balls'!" Her son can hardly speak, he's laughing so hard. "That's like nuts, right? Like your *dick*!" His mother, always the comedian. But the recovering terrorist is sitting on the sidewalk crying, *alligator tears*, as they're called, big fat drops that literally splat when they hit the pavement. I'm crying cats 'n' dogs, she thinks, and would laugh about the absurdity of it if she weren't so furious.

Then her husband is there rubbing her back, saying something soothing. She forces herself to bring his voice into focus and it's like surfing deep, dark water into sun-warmed light. "Foster's careful, he's a good kid, he knows better than to go on the road." Did she marry this man because of this delightful lack of ability to fret about the future or chew on the bones of the past? It's as if he's been genetically altered, the worry seed AWOL from his twist of DNA. It's all *hakuna matata* with him, her own Bobby McFerrin and Jeff Lebowski in one loving spoonful. This man who knows nothing of her dark heart, of the mercury semi-dormant in her veins, who deems what he thinks of as her "neurosis" charming at the best of times, and simply irritating at high tide.

Would her husband be willing to die for their son? Why didn't they talk about such things?

The boy, on the other hand, the boy is complicated. Complicates things. Raichu, evolved from Pichu and Pikachu, can store up to 100,000 electric volts in its cheeks and release them through its tail. Information she can use.

She's clipped the webbing between her left thumb and index finger with the secateurs. The blood is *pooling*, as it's called, but only she can see this. Her husband is gearing up for a joke, she can tell by how absent-minded his back strokes are getting. Her son dances around in front of them, an orange pressed to either side of his groin. "It's a bird, it's a plane, no, it's Super Vitamin C Balls!"

It's always the mother's fault. *As they say.*

Kurt from Vancouver: "I have this friend who seems determined to wreck this beautiful garden she's carefully built up over the years. I'm not the only one concerned. This self-destructive impulse threatens everything she holds dear."

The Gardening Dame: "And is there a word for this in the German, *Kurt*?"

Kurt from Vancouver: "Lucy, if you'd just—"

The Gardening Dame: "My advice, sir, is MYOB. Good fences make good neighbours, as they say. Next caller?"

GUNK SHOT

The man with the robotic voice has left a message. Tomorrow's appointment with the assistant manager of traffic calming measures has been cancelled due to the impending garbage and recycling strike. "We are seconding all senior municipal personnel in this time of crisis," he droned. *Bla-blah, bla-blah, bla-blah.* A bureaucrat's call to arms.

The recovering terrorist walks Houndoom along Victoria, where film trucks and trailers are lined up for blocks and McSpadden Park has been tricked out as a tent city for an episode of *Reaper.* A woman with what looks like an enormous tongue runs through the dilapidated tennis court, followed by a guy wielding a machete. He leaps the sagging net and there's a *boom!* and a feeble spray of black smoke. Houndoom yowls as if she wants to raise the dead. A man in a ball cap yells at a guy with pigtails, something like *one more premature blast and*—while about two dozen people holding coffee mugs and clipboards stand around doing nothing. The guy who plays Sock is covered in soot, mugging at onlookers in blackface, playing the machete like an air guitar.

She's reminded of the old "debates" they had back in their Chinatown squat about homemade explosives. Or "kitchen improvised munitions," as Leonard, a.k.a. Capt. Fudd, used to call them. This gave them a homey vibe, as if they were cooking up something for a potluck. Regan and Gerry treated it like a party game. "For $200. The seminal ingredient in urea nitrate." "What is semen?" Beep! "Oh sorry, Alex, I meant, 'What is urine?'" They were in love with the idea of using their own piss to blow things up.

"Metaphorically," said Damien, "it would be apt." Their target was the owner of a company that exported chlorine-filled diapers that had caused testicular cancer in third-world baby boys. The diapers were banned in Canada.

Plastic explosives? A Tampax cocktail? (They had experimented with that one—a tampon soaked in lighter fluid stuffed in a soy sauce bottle—and Regan had singed off his shaggy bangs. Leonard suggested the tampon be a used one for added symbolism. "We're not trying to make a *feminist* statement," Damien sneered.)

Eventually Carmen told them all to shut up. She was pouting. She had wanted them to chain themselves to a railway crossing in Poco, blocking a chlorine shipment from Sarnia, but Damien insisted Greenpeace had cornered the market on that tactic and that Carmen just wanted her tits splashed across the front page. It never occurred to the recovering terrorist at the time that this was most likely true.

But homemade plastic explosives today, the possibilities are endless. What did people do before the Internet, she wonders, offering up a prayer of thanks to Google. Add a glass jar of napalm—petrol and generic soap shards—for extra kick, one site advises. "Put it in a mason jar next to the explosive device for maximizing damage to the target."

The process of extracting potassium chlorate from household bleach is time-consuming and maddeningly multi-step, but her science degree at least taught her a modicum of patience with process, if not with life. Fractional crystallization, it's called. Science could be so poetic. "Craft project," she tells her husband when he asks about the smell coming from her workroom. "A surprise for everyone at Christmas—I think they're getting tired of updated copies of my *Grafting Perennials* classic."

She considers calling in her ultimatum from the phone booth at the corner of Hastings and Penticton, one of the few left in the entire city that hasn't been gutted or entirely disappeared overnight as if it had never existed. But they already have a record of her name, her request, *her particulars*, as they're called.

They issued an ultimatum way back then as well. Of course they did. Written on one of the company's own diapers filled with dog shit and deposited on the front steps of the captain of industry's Scarborough mansion. It never made the news, though. That should've been a warning to them. But. Maybe a maid removed it before anyone else could find it.

The family was supposed to be away that night at an out-of-town function, *intelligence* had it. Intelligence being Regan and Gerry. That should've been a warning as well. The daughter at a friend's. The "help"—god, she hated, still hates, that term—had the night off.

She had volunteered to do it—no, *insisted*. This was about children, the future. All the things she believed in. Damien gave her a big, soul-sucking kiss before she headed out. Carmen glared. Leonard saluted. Somewhere, making its way to the press, was their manifesto. She remembers how her legs were wobbling, almost comically, as if she were a drunken Olive Oyl. But she managed to move forward, a spastic walk before she started to run, shaky baby steps towards a better world.

The car will ignite as its wheels *crossed the line*. That much she knows.

If the driver has a passenger, well, that's collateral damage. And there is still the possibility the City will choose to see it her way. Hope, the thing with feathers.

Khan from Surrey: "My tomato plants have bites on them. Very little teeth. You think a big bug with a large mouth or a mice with a small mouth?"

The Gardening Dame: "Tell me, Khan, are you the kind of man who might tie his wife to a chair with gardening twine and set her on fire?"

MEAN LOOK

It feels great, this violent disgorging from the earth, the recovering terrorist thinks as she tears up blood grass by the roots with her bare hands. Her husband and son are off somewhere with The Hound. Next door there's the conscientious whirring click of a push mower. Across the street kids screech in someone's backyard as they get hosed down—yelling No! when they mean Yes! In the distance a train groaning through the cut, sirens, an ice-cream truck, crows. Summer in the city.

"We all missed you at group on Wednesday." Dieter squats beside her, his face so close she can see that his glasses are steaming up from the heat.

If this were a movie her next line would be: *What the %^*%$ are you doing here!?* But she just shakily stands as the chasm separating her two lives buckles, a cave-in of the Grand Canyon, burros with scratchy blankets on their backs scrambling for their lives, tourists wailing before clods of red earth pack mouths, ears, nostrils—sensory deprivation before oblivion.

"This has gone too far," Dieter says. No, it hasn't, Lucy thinks, not far enough. She could strike out with both hands, fury swipe, poison jab. "You don't even know who I am," she says instead.

"You are a bitch. You know that, right?" His eyes brim behind those distorting lenses. What did children call him at school? Four-eyes? Froggy? Fag? Did anyone recover from the nastiness of schoolyard taunts? Did he ever think about blowing up his tormentors? No, Dieter was a purist. He believed in causes, not himself. He believed in *people*.

Then there's Houndoom launching herself at Dieter, Foster straining at the other end of the leash. She introduces Dieter as a member of her book club. "Just checkin' out the 'hood," he tells Bruno, his eyes skittering like tropical fish.

Afterwards, Bruno says, "'Just checkin' out the 'hood?'"

"He's usually more articulate," Lucy tells him. "His German heritage, you know. All those million-dollar words."

"If he wasn't so obviously gay, I'd say that looked liked a lover's quarrel."

Foster squeezes between them, panic in his voice: "Hey, Mom! I just noticed Houndoom doesn't have any *balls*!"

If Hope is the thing with feathers (a sentiment that always puts Lucy in mind of the white feather floating through the treacle Forrest of that Tom Hanks movie), then what is Faith? Surely a thing with nasty thorns. Those who clutch at it remain bloodied but unbowed. Unlike so many in her circle—if you could call it a *circle*—she doesn't mock the faithful. Not after seeing what faith could do.

Lucy visited the dead girl's parents while she was pregnant. It was close to eleven years since that night. The girl would've been—what? Married and teaching Sunday school and awaiting her first child? A junior missionary in Honduras? A party girl downing tequila shots in her university dorm? A fledgling Olympic hurdler?

The house didn't have the look of a tomb or a shrine, as she'd imagined. It was cheerful in a perfectly ordinary way. On the mantel was the girl's picture, along with wedding photos of adult children and a grandchild holding up a lacrosse trophy. Lucy had pretended to be soliciting for a downtown mission for runaways and they actually invited her in off the doorstep and offered her tea. "Bless you," she said. "All other doors have been shut in my face." The odd locution she had borrowed from one of the nuns in *Lilies of the Field*.

Lucy had just wanted to witness how, *if*, someone could survive the death of a child. She looked at the photos and commented on the handsome family. "Two grandchildren?" she asked. No, their daughter, Anna, she was told. "She died when she was eight," the father said. "She was at her first sleepover. Nice people. There was a fire." They offered nothing more and she didn't ask.

Until that day she had thought of almost nothing for weeks but aborting the fetus, leaving Bruno, disappearing like Damien had, as if he'd never even been. What would that be like, to have never been?

"May I?" the mother asked. Not even showing at four months. It was as if the mother had a sixth sense. When the woman put her hand on her belly, that's when Lucy almost cracked. As she walked towards the door, only a kick from her baby to her navel, its first, kept her from turning around and, palms outward, dropping to her knees and begging, "Crucify me." But they would probably have forgiven her, which would have been even worse.

LAVA PLUME

In the distance, at the far end of the block, Lucy hears the car before she sees it. The tragically amplified bass, the pointless revving of the engine. She pictures the weasel-faced driver with his sparse chin hairs and Tasmanian Devil tattoo, a plump, scantily clad girl riding shotgun, egging him on. Lucy is all steady nerve and muscle, magma coursing through the chambers of her heart, churning through arterial walls.

But there's something else as well, something zooming by faster than it should. Faster than possible.

A cry of pure joy splits the air. A spinning wheel, spokes a whirl of silver glinting in the sun, fire tumbling overhead in an arc. Typhlosion, the flame-thrower Pokémon, its collar of fire a terrible beauty. The most evolved Pokémon of its kind. Anything touching it while it's aroused goes up in flames instantly.

The explosion is more intense than she thought it would be. Long minutes pass. The boy and his dog soon to emerge from a cloud of drifting ash like the survivors of 9/11. Ghostly grey, but upright, moving slowly as if reborn. Bloodied but unbowed. But no.

The boy a constellation. The Dog Star. The boy endless sky now.

The boy bread. The boy salt. The boy completed his final evolution.

And her?

Think about that old comic where the guy turns his wallet inside out and a few moths flutter out.

Think inside out. Think permanent flutter.

Or not. Try not to think about it too much.

That got name?

ACKNOWLEDGMENTS

There are many people I'm grateful to (and *for*) who lit a path for these stories—foremost among them Caroline "Kitten-with-a-Whip" Adderson and Charlotte Gill, fellow traveller, without whom this book might have remained a silent scream.

I owe oceans of thanks to Jackie Kaiser, agent extraordinaire and a great dame, for making everything easier; to Nicole Winstanley, my editor and publisher, who fizzes with vitality, grace, and intelligence, for her caring, intuitive editing; to the scarily smart and kind Nick Garrison, a redoubtable troubleshooter who saved me from some of my indulgences; to laser-eyed Shaun Oakey; and to the patient Sandra Tooze and rest of the crack team at the big flightless bird's Canadian headquarters.

Patty Jones, Lee Henderson, Neil Smith, Sarah Selecky, and Matthew J. Trafford provided jetpacks of psychic fuel. Timothy Taylor generously bequeathed me the name and DNA of Patrick Kakami.

Huge thanks are due to Gudrun Will, of *Vancouver Review*; Denise Ryan, of *The Vancouver Sun*; and John Burns, formerly of *The Georgia Straight*, three modern-day Medicis, and to the other editors, Sarah Fulford (*Toronto Life*), Jared Bland (*The Walrus*), Kim Jernigan (*The New Quarterly*), and Sylvia Legris (*Grain*), who so enthusiastically published some of these stories in earlier incarnations.

My astonishing students at UBC gave inspiration, while Capt. Andrew Gray maintained the lifeboats.

The words of so many writers inspire my fiction, but I'm particularly indebted here to the writings of Charles Darwin (for "Summer of the Flesh Eater") and to Joseph Conrad's *Heart of Darkness* (for "Mister Kakami").

Thank you to the Canada Council and the B.C. Arts Council for monies I'm sure they thought I'd squandered a million years ago.

And, as always, I am grateful to my friend Patrick Crean for enduring faith, and to my great loves John and Dexter Dippong for absolutely everything.